Home, Where the Wild Roses Grow

By Margaret Gadd Fowlkes

ISBN: 0-7596-7867-7 (E-book)
ISBN: 0-7596-7868-5 (Paperback)

Library of Congress Control Number: 2002090529

This book is printed on acid free paper.

Printed in the United States of America
Bloomington, IN

1stBooks - rev. 6/28/02

Acknowledgment:

Thanks to Vi and her bed making lesson!
To Alex-Book Cover

Dedicated:

To My Family

Up The hollow
Down the lane
Through the meadow
Home again.

The main characters are:
Great Grandfather Caleb
Great Grandmother Elizabeth
Grandmother Leah
Grandfather Luke
Jane and Luke
Mother and Daddy

My Great Grandparents

Great Grandfather Caleb

Before I go in my memories to this house, I need to recall my great grandparents on my Mother's side of the family tree, and then along with some of my Mother's and grandmother's remembrances of the happenings in their lives, including the red carpeted stairway as the story unfolds, just as they told me.

It seems there has been quite a lot of tragedy in my mother's and grandmother's lives. My mother's father and grandfather both met tragic fates. They were killed accidentally nearly a quarter century apart.

How I would love to have known each one. As it is, I've just caught a fleeting glimpse of both in what my mother and grandmother shared with me.

To begin, my great grandfather, Caleb, was in the Civil War, or as we now say, the War Between the States. He was captured by the Confederates, becoming a prisoner at Libby Prison in Richmond and moved to several other prisons in confederate states. The prisoners were not treated badly, except there was hardly enough food to feed everyone. Some died from malnutrition. One of those who died was my great grandfather's first cousin. His military records state he died from malaria, but my great grandfather said the starvation brought on his weakness and he succumbed to the dreaded disease.

Great Grandfather was released in March 1865, returning home to marry his sweetheart, Elizabeth. Sometime after their marriage, her mother and father moved to Missouri, selling their property to their new son-in-law for $2.00 an acre. Grandfather Caleb had a pension from the government, so he was pretty well off in those days.

The acreage he bought was a large estate, and he ran it like a gentleman farmer, owning many milk cows and sheep. Honey bee hives painted white set all around the house and garden, outside of the white palings I refer to later on in the telling of my story. Honey was a staple being on the table every day of the year.

My mother often reminisced about helping to milk the cows as a young girl, also tending to the sheep being sheared while they bleated sorrowfully to be turned loose, sending out distressing calls as if they were being harmed by the humans. We think of sheep as being quiet, but Mother said this was not always true. The wool was sold to companies who in turn carded it, making garments and other useful things, including carpets.

When the girls in the family were old enough for responsibilities, they were given a baby sheep to care for if the mother had deserted it, until it could go out on its own.

One of the daughters named her sheep Bridgette, often calling it to be fed and loved, after it was grown and eating in the fields with the others. Bridgette would come running when she heard her mistress's voice. It lived many years, always a family pet—sleeping on hay in its special manager in the old barn—hollow barn.

It was a year and two months after their marriage when my grandmother, Leah, was born, followed by several other children, boys and girls, some who also met tragic deaths after becoming adults.

Grandfather Caleb and Grandmother Elizabeth, knowing their *Bible*, named their first-born Leah. (Leah was the first-born daughter of Laban and was given to Jacob for his wife before he was allowed to marry Rachel; Genesis 29-25.)

When the children started coming along, the old house began to be a bit too small for their family, so a new one was built. And this is the house my mother was born in—also Luke, my brother, and myself, in the same bedroom upstairs on the left.

The upstairs bedrooms were huge, accommodating two double beds in each one, plus a large dresser with a drawer for each girl. The girls shared two beds, and the boys did the same in their room, hanging their clothes over the backs of chairs or on hooks driven into boards nailed to the walls. All the rooms, including the living room, had fireplaces with a chimney at each end of the house.

My mother often spoke of her Grandfather Caleb riding through the fields by the creek bank, driving his horse and buggy, checking on his animals, fences, and property.

When he was killed instantly, he was driving his horse and buggy across the railroad tracks, evidently not hearing the train whistle. My grandmother inherited the home after Grandfather Caleb's death, moving later to a smaller place, she and Uncle Otis. Mother and Daddy took the homeplace, the only home Luke and I had ever lived in.

Grandfather Caleb was so well known and highly regarded for his Christian principles and devotion to all that his death contributed to days of mourning that was unprecedented.

Because he loved his country, he had asked for his government pin to be placed in his lapel, and his wishes were kept at his death.

He was buried by his beloved Elizabeth, his son-in-law (my grandfather), his first cousin, three sons and four daughters, including Grandmother (in later years) in our old family cemetery, where we always decorated the graves with roses set down in blue glass jars.

One of Great Grandpa's and Elizabeth's lovely daughters, my great aunt, also met death tragically by train. It was winter and her husband had died two weeks before. She had gone by train to the city to have his will probated. On her return, she got off the train not far from her home and began walking up the track like she had always done. The wind was very strong and it flipped her fur collar up around her head, making it impossible to hear the train bearing down on her.

Several witnesses saw what was happening and lamented to themselves, "Why doesn't she get off the tracks?" She simply did not hear the warning whistle. Her sister, Ann, the youngest in the family, was staying with her and the children. That very morning before going into town, she accidentally caught her apron on fire. She stated, "Oh, Ann," in a distraught voice, "What would the children do if anything should happen to me?"

I was five years old, and what I remember about that terrible time was Daddy bringing the newspaper home with enlarged headlines, "Woman Killed by Train" and Grandma saying, "Not Sister! Not Sister!"

The children were well taken care of, but they missed their once happy close home life with their mother and father. Four other daughters died from cancer and heart problems, one of which looked very much like my grandmother. They were both short and a little on the round side. Later in telling my story, I talk about the great uncles in my great grandparents' family.

Great Grandmother Elizabeth

Great Grandmother Elizabeth was a wonderful, caring person, going all over the countryside helping others. She would drive her little spring-board wagon, taking food to the sick, preparing meals, or helping with preserving of the harvest, and even delivering babies.

There were no funeral parlors in those days, and oftentimes she helped to lay their friends and neighbors out once they had died. She, along with other ladies, would bathe the deceased, comb their hair, dress them in an appropriate outfit, and stay with the family. Several of the women would then come by and start preparing food for the relatives who would be coming to stay until after the funeral. A pine casket was generally the only mode of burial back then.

Grandfather Caleb at the same time would go in his own buggy or on horseback to let all the neighbors know of the death of a dear friend or relative.

Not long after one of these incidents, Grandmother Elizabeth began running a fever.

My grandmother told me about her mother's illness while in one of her reminiscent moods.

"After two days of high fever, Grandfather Caleb summoned the doctor. Soon after, she began to get better, much to the relief of all of us. For a month or so, she seemed well, and then the fever returned again. Upon close examination, the doctor informed Grandfather Caleb that Elizabeth had breast cancer.

We were all so alarmed, for we knew it meant certain death. She lived almost a year with agonizing pain before the Lord saw fit to take her home with him. She died in the other room at the top of the stairs on the right. Dying suddenly one day, it was ruled she passed away from a brain hemorrhage.

"There was great mourning for our mother," Grandma said. "She was a lady, a lovely lady, helping anyone who needed help.

It didn't matter if they were rich or poor. If they needed her, she was there."

Grandmother Elizabeth was buried in the family cemetery, followed by Grandfather Caleb several years later, where Luke, my brother and I used to help Grandma and Mother in keeping of the graves on decoration day many years afterward.

Grandfather Caleb was a devoted husband. He never remarried after Elizabeth's death, often remembering little things in their lives and how very short the years had been.

And now I begin my story of *Home, Where the Wild Roses Grow*.

Prologue

Trevor, my husband, had gone his way and I started up the path to where my home place used to be. The lane held weeds and burrs; the trees had grown over on either side, looking much like a canopy or a huge umbrella holding vines and leaves.

It was with some kind of expectation I had envisioned before I came to the end of the path, but when I reached it nothing was there; just an empty space. I turned around twice, thinking I must be in the wrong place or lost. I've taken the little road way up to the old barn instead of the one leading to where the house used to set, I thought.

Suddenly I realized I wasn't lost, nor had I taken the wrong way. This is it. This is where my home used to be. A feeling of sadness and despondency swept over me like an ocean wave, nearly knocking me down with shock. I wanted to run and cry out, "No, No!" This couldn't have happened to our home.

Along with this sad, helpless feeling in my heart, a chill engulfed me as I tried to get myself situated into a time and age of long ago but yet still mingled with the present. I felt a tingling running from my spine down through the back of my legs. For a moment, or was it two, my heart nearly stopped as I looked around me.

Then my mind began whirling trying not to accept what I already knew, but couldn't grasp it right now.

<u>Home, Where the Wild Rose Grow</u>

As I stood looking at the empty space where the old home used to stand, it was almost as if I could hear Grandma saying, "You're just bustin'to cry, ain't ya honey?" She always laughed and said I got more out of crying than any person she ever knew. She was sure I was pretty close to being 98 percent water.

It took just about everything inside of me to hold back the tears. But I'd made up my mind not a tear was to fall to the ground this day.

Luke, my brother, had called and informed me the old home place had burned to the ground. It happened one night in a terrible electric storm.

"Must have been hit direct," one of the neighbors had said to me earlier. "I'll miss it," he continued. "It was a landmark in so many ways and to so many people. I sure hate it, Miss Jane."

"Things have to change, I suppose," I replied—knowing it was true but not really believing it—even though there were changes around me every day. There are some things you want to hold on to—never to let go, and this old house where it used to be, as I remembered, was one of those things, I thought.

My parents could never bring themselves to sell the home place, always hoping their only daughter would one day come back home with her family and take up residence where she had grown up.

We, Trevor, the children, and I, never had a permanent place we could call home. Now the kids were almost grown and on their own more than we wanted to admit. We were searching for the right decision; had discussed often the possibility of returning to our roots one day, never dreaming something like this would happen.

When Luke told our parents the old home was gone, they both cried at first. Luke hoped this wouldn't keep us from returning home to live, he stated to them.

"That will be Jane and Trevor's decision, not ours," Daddy had said. Mother was in agreement with him and replied, "Yes, that will be their decision. I want them to be happy wherever they live."

They had lived long enough to accept whatever change each day brought to them, whether it be good or bad. And one of those changes was when our parents closed up the old house and moved to a smaller place several years before not far from Luke.

Trevor and I had driven from our home to the mountains to check on the property after the fire. He had recently retired from the military and we were more or less fancy free.

Trevor must have known I would need some time to myself. "You go ahead, Jane, and decide what you need to do. I'm going to check the fences and the boundary lines. I'll come back in a couple of hours up that way when I finish." Trevor was like that. He had a built in knowledge of how people would feel about things, or that they might need to be alone to think things through. He never offered any advice. He just said, "I'll see you in a couple of hours, Jane."

The old home was gone, but the steps and chimneys remained. The wooden steps had been replaced years ago with cement ones. Steps have such a purpose—always leading to something good or sometimes bad—regardless of which way you're going whether it be up or down—these steps led us to something that could never be destroyed or diminished either by an act of God or man.

As I continued in my thoughts, I climbed the steps once again and it felt as if I was coming home. Just like it felt when I had been away a long time. I could see myself running up the steps and into Mother's arms waiting for me when we came home on furlough. And Daddy not saying much, just beaming so glad to see his daughter, son-in-law, and grandkids. If only there was a door to open, but of course there wasn't. I came back down and stood where our home used to be. My mind began to retrace each room, space and time bringing back its own memory of long ago.

<u>The Front Porch</u>

Now just about here would be the front porch, I thought, as I marked it off with the toe of my shoe. What better place to start than right here on the old porch where our family had always gathered to discuss the everyday happenings in our lives, or even the future hopeful happenings to come. Everybody had a front porch back then. No one ever built a house in the early 1900s or before on up to the 1940s without a porch. There would be a swing, a homemade bench, and a chair or two. If several came to visit at one time, an extra chair was brought out from the kitchen. We kids sat there on the porch with our feet hanging down, wiggling our toes, listening to the conversations, giggling and acting shy with one another.

"A front porch is a necessity," Grandma always said. There are certain people you want only on your porch and no further, such as the long-winded, quarrelsome person. You must always be civil to people, even if you don't care too much for them. But the porch is as far as you can let them venture."

With a slight stir of the wind, I thought about the wooden trellis that was once nailed to the east end of the porch. The climbing vine covered it entirely, not letting any sun in during the hot summer months. Only a gentle breeze could break through the big vine leaves. How heavenly that breeze was. The vine would come to life with its tiny pink flowers, rendering all its beauty until the fall season, when it would die back into the ground, never to show itself again until springtime.

Talk then was about gardens and Mrs. Raines' new babies— seems she had one every year. "Don't know why these people keep having babies," I said more than one time. "They can barely feed the ones they have." Mother would reply, "The good Lord will provide, Jane"—always her standard answer. And somehow those kids did survive—got all grown up, married, and started the same process their parents had done. Mother was right; you do what you know is the correct thing and God does provide. I guess that's the way life is supposed to be, I pondered once again.

In the summer, Momma came out in the afternoons to peel her potatoes for supper. If they were new potatoes, she scraped them. She never sat in the swing or chairs but on the porch itself with her feet on the top step. She would scrape or peel and look out over the yard bursting with color, or the fields turning green with new life.

Most of the time I'd be sitting in the swing sewing on a dress I was trying to put together or embroider. Mother didn't like to sit and sew. "I'd rather be out with nature," she'd say. "Why make a dress when you can go buy one. Besides, I don't have time."

She did the milking, churning, and looking for hens' nests, especially the guineas. They were always hiding their eggs out in the tall grass. I think they really played hide and go seek with Mother. They were just a bunch of watch dogs to me. They would let you know when someone strange was coming up in the yard. Their clucking and screeching would bring you out to see where the trouble was.

Yes, the old porch had lots of functions. How well I remember the summer I got terribly sick and "out of my head" like the old timers would say, vomiting night and day. Mother and Daddy made me a cot out here because it was too hot in the house.

Grandma came and saw the condition I was in and decided to take matters into her own hands. "This child," she said, "will have to have something in her stomach or she ain't goin' to live. Now you sit with her while I go gather them catnip tea leaves from under them rose bushes right there." She meant the rose bushes in our front yard, which held dozens of every size and color.

She made the tea from the little yellow and green leaves, adding a bit of honey to it. It still tasted awful. Even now cold chills run over me when I think about that, but I was too sick to care. Daddy held my head up while she spooned it down me. I began to get better and slept around the clock.

Our neighbor, Opal, came and said the minister had held special prayer for me. It felt so good to know that people had put up a petition to God to spare my life.

Then I thought about Grandma's tea. I finally reasoned it all out. I decided it was God and Grandma. God can't help in peoples' lives unless he has grandmas and grandpas to see that his work is done. So, Grandma made the tea, the people prayed, and God got busy and made me well. Maybe I would have gotten well without either one, but I wouldn't want to risk it. I owed a lot to God and Grandma.

While stirring the dirt with my shoe, a smile came to my face as I remembered my first kiss was about right here. After all these years, whenever I think about it, I get goose bumps. It was so sweet, and I thought it all had been spoiled at that moment by my actions.

We were having a protracted revival meeting at our church. Along with several others, Trevor walked me home after church was over. On that special night, we went up the steps to the porch. Then Trevor said, "Well, goodnight Jane." I guess he thought he was supposed to kiss me goodnight since I had allowed him to walk me home. I secretly thought he might, but when he did, it took me quite by surprise. I didn't know how to react so I just kissed him back, grabbed open the door, and ran into the parlor, slamming it behind me. I stood looking out the window that was curtained in lace, not wanting him to see my face. All the windows had lace curtains hanging to the floor except the door, and it had different shades of colored glass.

Trevor stood there for a moment looking in my direction, but not seeing me through the window covering, still with a surprised look on his face. He turned and began bouncing down the steps. I could see him running like a deer through the yard, when then much to my surprise, he jumped the gate and kept running.

"He can't wait to get away. What will he think of me?" I cried to myself.

I could have slapped my own face. Why did I do such a thing, I asked myself a hundred times that night while tossing and turning before I finally fell into a restless sleep.

My first thought upon awakening the next morning was that Trevor would never look at me again. I moped around the house until Mother sensed something was wrong. "What's the matter with you, Jane?" I fell into her arms, explaining what I had done the night before and knowing somehow it just wasn't right. "Trevor will never look at me again," I sobbed over and over.

"Pshaw!" Mother said. "I don't see nothing wrong with it. Girls have a right to express themselves too. Now he knows where he stands. He knows you like him too, Jane" she said, with a little smile on her face. "I bet his heart has been aflutter all day, and he can't wait to walk you home again tonight."

That did little to salve my guilty conscience, but she was right, for somehow our friends all knew Trevor and I were sweethearts. From that moment on, it was a given among our peers. Don't ask me how they knew. They just knew. When he came into church that evening, they began making a place for him beside me. I looked at Trevor, knowing at that instant I would never love another person. Somehow I knew he felt the same about me.

I can still laugh, remembering our wedding day. After Trevor kissed me when the minister said, "You can now kiss your bride," I looked over at Mother, giving her a wink, reached up and kissed my husband, while the whole congregation laughed and applauded.

It was a little secret between Mother and I. I'm sure Daddy knew that secret too—for Mother always told Daddy everything.

At supper the same evening of the day I had been so wretched, Daddy was in a jovial mood. He talked all through the meal. He said Lucious, our neighbor, was really impressed by Trevor. He had hired him for the summer and that boy could really turn out the work. He'd never seen a young man work as hard and steady as that young man had that day. "Yes sir, that boy will be a fine catch for some young lady one of these days," Daddy added. Then he caught my eye and said, "Ain't you just a little bit sweet on Trevor, honey?"

"Oh Daddy," I replied, while inside my heart was pounding for joy. Mother and I looked at one another remembering our conversation.

Trevor's family were English through and through. They spoke in Old English mostly—their sentences broken and sometimes kind of hard to understand. Their words were foreign and sounded strange and funny to others; like the word "<u>it</u>" was pronounced with an "<u>h</u>" and spoken like "<u>hit</u>."

When Trevor's father would be telling of some incident, he always said, "I ope to tell ya," instead of "hope to tell you." This embarrassed Trevor quite a lot until he was studying Old English and he realized why his parents spoke in the way they did. After that, it was never embarrassing to him again.

"I kind of like it," he told me. He brought *The Canterbury Tales* home for his parents to read, and what joy they had reading and discussing them.

I loved his parents, having known them all my life. They raised a big family in a two-story home almost like ours.

Still standing on the porch in my dreams, I turned looking toward the front of the yard. "That's where the wild roses grew," I said out loud.

I'd forgotten about the wild roses. Down from Momma's garden you could find them on a little terrace from the main yard. I could see their tiny buds and beautiful petals which opened quickly—showing mauves, and deep, deep pinks—and they were still there—surviving all these years. The fire that burned the house had not reached them. I never knew why they were there in that certain place. They just grew wild—no one planted them. They were there for us to enjoy, I know now.

Where the wild roses grew was the special spot for my playhouse and see saw. Oh, the happy hours Beulah Belle, my best friend, and I spent pretending we were married, carrying our baby dolls in little homemade blankets going on a train trip.

The reason Beulah Belle and I always played we were going on a train was because when I was seven-years-old, Grandma took a trip to Hot Springs, Arkansas, by train.

Her arthritis flared up, and she could hardly get out of bed some mornings. Sitting down was almost as bad. Mother would have to go evenings especially to help her to bed. Uncle Otis, Mother's brother, was able to get her up at morning time, taking care of her needs during the day, but Mother did the taking care of evenings.

Someone in Grandma's acquaintances mentioned the baths at Hot Springs, Arkansas, which they had heard about. Grandma could see she wasn't improving so decided to make arrangements to go.

I can remember getting up early and Mother saying that this was the day Grandma had to go on a big long train to Hot Springs, Arkansas, and she hoped she'd get better from the hot water baths there. I wondered why they didn't just heat some bath water for Grandma, mentioning this to my parents.

Mother and Daddy had a big laugh over what I had said, and later somehow it made the morning seem a little more cheerful, rather than a dark cloud hanging over us, Mother told Grandma when we picked her up. My imagination had run wild, for Daddy tried to explain to me how the water bubbled all the time, kept hot by underground springs of heat, but all I could think of was little stoves underneath the water, burning all the while, never going out from tiny sticks of wood being fed by little underground people.

I wasn't the only one to believe there was someone or something under the water keeping it warm, for Grandma learned while there that our native Americans believed a Great Spirit resided under the springs and his breath was the steam rising above the water.

We reached the train station and even were allowed to go on board to get Grandma settled in for her long trip. There was lots of huggin' and kissin', lots of do's and don'ts from Mother to Grandma.

"I'll be good," Grandma said, with her big smile. "Just you take care of these youngins' and Otis while I'm gone."

It was cold the morning she left, and she wore her black karakul wool coat with its tiny little curl loops stitched all over it. This type of wool was from a certain black sheep of Asia taken from the new lambs of this breed. They were very popular back then. The collar came down over her shoulders, almost cape-like. That was to be the last time we were to see her wearing it, for on her return trip, she left it in the train station in Hot Springs.

Sometimes in my memory that old train whistle stands out, as well as the chugging and sputtering just before it pulled out with Grandma on it while we four stood holding hands while tears were making a headway down my cheeks.

I don't remember leaving the station, but I do remember that we all went shopping. Later for lunch, Daddy ordered hamburgers—my very first hamburger—not on a bun but on plain thick bread. No tomato or lettuce but a big slice of onion and pickle. I can't remember if Luke had ever had one before.

There were lots of firsts that day—my first time at a train station, my first shopping in the big downtown city, and my first hamburger. What a day to remember for such a little girl.

Soon we began receiving post cards from Grandma. "Feeling much better," she wrote on each one. "Miss the children," was on the ones sent to Mother. "The springs are like something out of a fairy tale," she wrote to Luke and me. "I think about what Jane said and laugh." "Have met people from different places." "Everyone so friendly." "Love, Grandma."

One post card had a beautiful scene of buildings with huge trees. On it was written, "Army and Navy Hospital, Hot Springs Mountain and Bath House Row."

She told us later that veterans from the war between the states and World War I came there for rest and water therapy.

I'm sure she must have thought of her dad serving in the Civil War and how he suffered from infestation of rats, bed bugs, from lack of nourishing food, and creature comforts while being shuffled from one prison to another for two years as a prisoner of war.

Grandma was there for six weeks. When she returned, she was a different person, spry as could be, walking with a spring in her step, claiming the baths had been wonderful, along with the experience of uplifting her soul, at such a distressful time in her life.

When Grandma stepped from the train, we were right there to greet her, giving big hugs and kisses once again. "You'll never know how much I missed all of you. I'm so glad for the opportunity to have gone, but I never want to be away from you again."

"The only thing to mar my trip is leaving my beautiful coat in the train station. I can always buy a new coat, so I'm not going to cry over spilt milk, but I want you to know that's the end of my travelin'."

"Now I can't wait to get home and see my house and farm. I hope you're plannin' to have turnip greens and cornbread for supper," she said to my mother, not in a questioning way but just a statement, as if she already knew what Mother had prepared.

Grandma had taken time to find tiny stones, pasting them on cardboard for Luke and me. She helped us to identify these "gems" as she called them. They were very pretty, especially glistening in the sun, as we pretended they were gold and silver, while we bartered back and forth.

Grandma kept her word for sure. The only places she went after that was to church, or a funeral, or to the little country store. Luke and I most always went with her to the store, for it meant a cold drink or a loose fig newton cookie for us. Sometimes we got both. But Grandma's arthritis seemed to disappear, which we were all thankful for, including Grandma.

But Luke and I never did a pretend train trip—only Beulah Belle and I. When we tired of playing grown up being on a train, we'd hop up on the see saw, riding up and down, up and down, singing:

"See Saw Margery Daw.

Jack shall have a new master.

He shall make but a penny a day.

'Cause he can't work any faster."

In my mind's eye and ear, I could see and hear our laughter combined with the creaking of the plank we used to sit on, Beulah Belle and I, as we see-sawed day after day in the summer months. With tears starting to form, I said out loud, "Oh, Beulah Belle, I loved you so."

Trying to hold back the tears, I kept thinking I can't let myself be sad, so I turned back toward where the porch used to be. I must go on to all those wonderful times in this wonderful old house, I thought to myself.

Leaving the porch and the wild roses in my memories, I slowly moved to the parlor in my thoughts using my shoe to guide me as I marked off this fancy room in another time and era.

Margaret Gadd Fowlkes

<u>The Parlor</u>

Our parlor had several windows, one on each side of the door and two on each outside wall. As I said before, they were covered with lace curtains. Mother ordered them from Sears & Roebuck Company. These were the style of the day. Most everyone had lace curtains either at the windows or on the front door.

The door was a beautiful oak, hewn by hand. It held an octagon shaped window with stained glass of many hues, which oftentimes was like a prism. Red, yellow, blue, and pink colors seeped through, sending different shades into the parlor, sometimes reaching into the living room, depending on the time of day and year. My brother and I would run through the room fast so no color could light on us. But that was an impossible feat we discovered early on. Still, it never kept us from trying over and over, I remembered.

The beautiful door had been removed years before, replaced by a plain wooden one, while the original door was kept at Trevor's mom's house in one of the upstairs bedrooms. In fact, we had divided the furniture at the same time. Luke kept my pieces stored in the upper part of the barn until we could decide where we would be living after Trevor's discharge from the service.

We had lived in many places including overseas stations. It was always in our minds that we would one day come home to live.

The children seemed to be adjusted wherever we lived, but one time I remember my heart nearly breaking for our child, as well as for myself, when he asked me a haunting question.

They were playing in a tree in our yard when my second born said to me, "Momma, when are we going back to Mom's side of the world?" They always called my mother "Mom."

I was so taken back by the question that for a few seconds, I couldn't answer. I finally did, my eyes brimming with tears. I told him it would probably be a long time, but we would go back to Mom's side of the world to live one day. He was satisfied with the answer and went scrambling farther up the tree with the others. But the question lingered with me for a long, long time.

Luke, my brother, was nearly two years older than I. We did just about every crazy thing there was to do. We swung from the grapevines that grew in the tall oaks and swam in the creek. Since I was Jane, we would pretend he was Tarzan. Even now when he calls, his first words will be, "Me Tarzan, you Jane?" We climbed the hills gathering nuts in the fall or blackberries in the summer.

There I go again rambling, but back to the parlor.

All the kids in our neighborhood congregated in our home, especially the parlor. There were all kinds of games to play besides having the old Victrola and the upright piano where everybody took turns playing chopsticks sooner or later. A little day bed served as a couch. There were brass railings on the back and sides with lots of pillows to caress or plump up while sitting. A certain small pillow was used when we played, "I Send My Ship A'Sailing." There was this big square table that sat to the left side, holding crossword puzzles, dominoes, checkers, Chinese checkers, and card games. The card games were played by the young and old, such as Rook and Cribbage.

We sometimes teased Daddy, asking him if he was allowed to come into the parlor when he and Mother were courting.

"Oh yes," he would reply "Your mother and I would wind up the old Victrola and play some of the records that were popular then."

Daddy and Mother often played those old records for us while they sang the lyrics, harmonizing quite well. I remember two of the really old songs were "I'm only a Bird in a Gilded Cage," and another we liked was called "Hand me Down My Walking Cane, I'm Going to Leave on that Midnight Train."

Still thinking about Daddy and what he told me one day here in the old parlor certainly caused me to have a different outlook on life from then on.

The story began when I was fifteen—the time of life when I thought I owned the whole world and everything in it. Besides having wonderful friends, I had a handsome brother who all the girls adored.

On this particular day I came to Mother on the front porch asking if I could go swimming with some others down at Willoby's Pond Creek.

"I don't know the people who gather there, Jane, so I can't let you go; besides, the road is very narrow there, you could possibly be run down by a car."

"But I'll be careful," I replied.

"The answer is no, Jane."

I asked again, and then again, and still the answer was no. Finally Mother turned away starting into the house. I knew then what she had said was final and that's when I retorted back to her.

"You know, Mother," I said in a flippant tone, for a long time now I've begun to believe you and Daddy adopted me. You are afraid I'll run away if I ever find out the whole truth. That's why you won't let me do things I want to do."

Her back was to me by then, and I'm sure I couldn't have stabbed her any worse had I had a knife, for she paused a brief second not saying "nay nor yea." She opened the screen door, going on in through the house to the kitchen. I could have cut my tongue out as I thought upon the thing I had said.

Getting up from the porch swing, I sheepishly went to my bedroom, stopping to look at the pictures on the mantel, while tears formed in my eyes. I laid down and began to cry a little for hurting Mother's feelings from what I had said.

Looking for something to occupy my time, I spied an old newspaper there on my bedside table, opened it up to read the funnies, and wouldn't you know the very first one on the page was Little Orphan Annie. This brought a smile to my face, replacing that awful feeling I had imposed upon myself.

I got up, went outside, finding my scarf to embroider and was busy the rest of the afternoon. Soon Mother brought her potatoes out to be peeled, or was it scraped, since it was still springtime.

We talked as if nothing had ever happened, while I was pretty sure Mother had forgotten and forgiven her daughter for saying something she knew wasn't true.

I had dismissed the incident from my mind until two days later while sitting in the parlor listening to Tommy Dorsey's band on the radio, Daddy suddenly came in and sat down beside me, while turning down the radio at the same time.

"Little girl," he began, "your mother tells me you might think you were adopted. Is that what you said?" he asked.

"Yes Sir, that's what I said," I replied. Before I could say another word, he continued.

"Let me assure you that you are not adopted, for I saw you come into this world and you came feet first. I only hope when you become a mother you'll never experience that kind of suffering."

I was shocked for a couple of reasons. Besides it being so sudden without any warning, Daddy had never said anything to me about how people are born, and I had never thought that you could come feet first. In fact, I had never given it much thought at all. I was just here, here in this old house that I loved so much.

After the shock wore off a little, I began to scramble for words, letting him know I was just mad when I said what I did to Mother. Finally I was able to come up with a good answer that I knew would somehow please Daddy and make everything right again.

"Daddy, I felt so bad after saying that to Mother that day, I went to my room, and the first thing I saw was Aunt Jane's picture on the mantel. And you know, just like you said, I'm the spittin' image of her for sure."

Never was the subject brought up again. Even now I shudder to think how I could have had such a ridiculous idea, but as I said, I was fifteen, and sometimes when you're fifteen, you do and say lots of crazy things. Funny, I would remember that incident on this day while my thoughts are in this old room.

Several of Dad's friends played Rook in the parlor. As I got older, I liked the game too. It was always fun to get the old crow and be able to use it at the appropriate time. When our children came along, they knew lots of games and read books, continuing to play Rook like we did in our younger years.

I stood for a moment thinking about the children, and what they had said to me when I told them I was going home to check things out. Each one was concerned, expressing their thoughts and feelings about whether I should go or not.

"It will be alright," I had told each one. "Sooner or later I have to go see about the property anyway."

"It will be different Momma," one of them had said. "I don't think you should get upset."

What wise children I had. They knew, too, how the tears fell abundantly in a crisis. I also knew how tears can help wash away things you can't do anything about. After a good cry, I could always figure out my next move, but I had said to myself not a tear was to fall to the ground this day.

Thinking about our children, my husband, Luke and I, Mother and Daddy and how things used to be, I entered the space that was once our living room.

<u>The Living Room</u>

There was no door between these two rooms I remembered, as I stepped from the parlor into the living room in my thoughts. Big and square it was—must have been 20 x 20. Funny, I never measured it. I bet Mother knew and of course Daddy would know.

Two large rocking chairs sat in front of the fireplace, winter and summer, one for Momma and one for Daddy. What I remember most was Momma reading to us in this room about some happening in the world that not one of us could understand, while Luke and I perched on each arm of her chair. The chair we sat on belonged to my great grandparents. Mother and Daddy still use it to this day in their new smaller home.

The time that stands out in my memory when Mother cried with tears running down her cheeks was the time she read to us about the Lindbergh baby being kidnapped and later found dead. She then gathered Luke and me close to her and rocked us for a few minutes in that overstuffed chair while Daddy looked on. He then got up, giving us a pat on the head, removing his glasses, wiping his eyes on a big cotton handkerchief before going out to sit on the front porch and ponder this thing that Mother had just read.

It's strange how we can feel love that was given years before, but that's how it was then in our family and my family now, and still is in families everywhere, I'm sure.

It was almost like a ritual every Sunday morning when Dad wound the old clock which belonged to his grandfather. It sat on the mantel, which was right in the middle of the living room. It's odd how you learn to sleep through all the bongings during the night. If Mother, Daddy, and Luke were gone and I was alone, I can remember listening to the ticking—not another sound—just tick tock, tick tock. It would nearly drive me mad. In later years, I would switch on the radio and listen to some popular swing bands, just so I couldn't hear the old clock ticking. Now, I think it would be soothing to the soul to once again hear the ticking of an old fashioned clock. Mother and Daddy kept their old faithful time piece for their new apartment, and he still winds it once every week.

Large pink roses dominated the walls in here. Daddy would always take a day off and help Mother put up the colorful wall covering. The paper had to be trimmed, the roses or lines matched before cutting strips to hang. A thick starch was made and pasted on the back side of each panel with a brush about nine inches wide.

In this room, linoleum was laid. It could be very cold to the feet on frosty mornings. Mother crocheted for years it seemed on a big oval rug. Even now I could picture her. After the evening chores were done, she sat tearing or cutting strips of material. Then she would crochet them together until it was finally finished. The rug was so pretty, with lots of blues mingled together.

I can also remember how for many a summer, that old rug would have to be taken up and put on the clothesline, then beaten with a broom until not a mite of dust came from it. I laugh when I remember how I'd flail that thing with the broom in one hand while at the same time be reading a book while holding it in the other. Mother would tell me, ever so often, leaning out the kitchen window, "At the rate you're going, you'll be all day getting that rug cleaned."

Luke worked with Dad in the fields most of the time in the summer until the war came, and then Dad went to work in a war plant. I think everybody's life changed then. Everything was the same, but yet it was not the same. We got up each morning, we did the chores, we ate, and we listened to the radio for each tiny scrap of war news. We counted our ration stamps. We bought certain groceries and sometimes shoes if we had enough stamps. We talked with neighbors about the war, the crops, and the boys. We came home. We wrote letters. We went to bed. I could see Mother and Daddy tired from worry and work.

It was lonely—oh, so lonely. All the neighbor boys had gone off to war, including Luke and Trevor.

As soon as Luke and Trevor graduated, they were off to join the army. They knew they would soon be drafted so they got a jump on the draft. They were together almost two years and then separated. Luke went overseas first, and then Trevor.

I was still Trevor's sweetheart. He came home several times before I graduated and called me every chance he got.

I looked around in the space allotted for the living room and stood where our phone used to set. It was placed on one of those little tables that looked as if it had another half somewhere. Then one evening Trevor called from camp. He told me he had a thirty day furlough and would I please marry him. I was so happy to know I was going to be Mrs. Trevor Turnor that I fairly shouted into the phone, "Yes, yes!"

Right here is where Mother and I planned my wedding. It was actually planned over the phone. When Trevor asked me to marry him, he made it clear he wanted us to get married as soon as he got home, for thirty days would go awfully fast, he had said.

He came on Friday, and we were married the next evening in Trevor's and my church. That's when I looked back at Mother and winked, reaching up, kissing him.

I wore my mother's wedding dress, the same dress Grandmother had made for Mother's wedding. It was a white voile with a large rounded collar. The dress had long sleeves which fastened with two pearl buttons. There were snaps down the side with a belted waistline. The hem was doubled with an extra piece of material folded over and sewed down by hand all around. The slip, white satin that went with the dress, was also handmade. Tiny pink embroidered flowers in two rows were around the neck and hem. I carried my mother's white Bible with a small bouquet of tiny flowers held together with pink and white ribbon. Pink and white flowers surrounded my wide-brimmed hat with flowing ribbons the same color, falling down the back onto my shoulders.

In my pierced ears were Grandmother's earrings. She gave them to me for a wedding present, which I still wear real often. I hope some day to give them to my daughter. Maybe she will wear them on her wedding day as I did not so many years ago. They were made of copper, shaped like tiny horseshoes.

How well I remember the torture I went through to have my ears pierced when I was twelve. "Once they get well, Jane, you'll be able to wear beautiful earrings," she said as she bathed my earlobes with warm salt water, while the tears flowed. "I have some special earrings for you," she told me then. They were beautiful and special.

"These are for you to wear on your wedding day. Your grandfather gave them to me just before we were married. Now they are yours." I looked at Grandmother, remembering what she had told me about Grandpa when I was not quite in my teens. I'm sure she was remembering her wedding day so long ago that I try to capture later in my story. How lucky I was to have such a loving and caring family. I was so happy and yet sad to know Trevor would be gone in such a short time.

Trevor was simply handsome in his army uniform. He was beaming the whole evening. I think I shall remember forever the moment he placed this gold band on my finger, as I now looked down at it once again, moving it back and forth, thinking about Trevor and our family.

Thank goodness for pictures. Cameras were not popular or plentiful as they are now, but we do have a few pictures. My cousin had an old Brownie one and made several photos of us cutting our wedding cake and tossing my bouquet. How I still cherish those pictures.

Those thirty days went by awfully fast, just as Trevor had said. Grandma let us use her house while she and Otis stayed with Mom and Dad. "You need to be by yourselves. They can put up with us for a month or so," she said with a big smile on her sweet face.

I think they all enjoyed having Grandma underfoot for awhile. Daddy liked to tease her about getting married again, but she always had a reply to Daddy. "You're not ever goin' to get rid of me. You can mark that down in your little book right now." I can hear Daddy laughing. How he enjoyed getting her riled up, just for the fun of it.

In the days that followed, we walked the farm over holding hands while making plans for our future. "When the war is over, Jane, I'll come back here and we'll build us a house close to our folks." It didn't work out that way, I remembered. After the war was over, jobs were scarce, and he rejoined in a few months that took us far away from our dreams. Now here we are, 20 years from those moments. How could time go so fast, I wondered.

And then those thirty days were up, and Trevor was gone. It would be two years before he was home again. How I missed him and Luke. I wrote Luke every week and Trevor just about every day.

Daddy worked long hours, making war materials, still running the farm in his spare time. I went to work out of high school for a small company. Mother kept busy with her guineas and chickens, running the house and helping Daddy with the farm, while looking after Grandma, as she always had done for several years.

I had gone back to work after Trevor left, keeping myself busy. It was right after lunch one day, nearly four weeks after he had left, that I felt nauseated. It dawned on me after the second wave of nausea that I must be pregnant. When I was sure, I wrote Trevor the news. He was well on his way overseas when he received my letter.

He wrote back as soon as he could. "I'm the happiest fellow on board this ship, but I just wish I was home with you. Oh, Jane, what has happened to our world? You'll have lots of good help with your parents, and my parents and Grandma. Please take care of yourself and keep those letters coming."

I worked until two months before the baby came. Things sure have changed, I thought. Nowadays, most women work right up to delivery time.

What fun it was to plan for your firstborn. Daddy went up into the attic and retrieved the little iron bed that had been in the family for years. Mother repainted it white. "That's the one bed she always left white," I laughed to myself. We all knew how Mother wielded a paint brush on all the iron beds come spring every year.

Daddy put the bed in the upstairs bedroom on the left, the room in which Mother, Luke, and myself had been born. Our plans were for little Trevor (if it was a boy) to be born here also. It was still Luke's bedroom, but for now we wanted the baby to be born there. His room would be waiting for him when he got back from the war. But most times in birth and death we don't have any control.

I didn't make it upstairs the day he was born. As a matter of fact, I was standing right here in this spot when the news about Trevor came.

I was taking an afternoon nap when I was awakened by Mother's voice saying, "Please, come on in to the living room." I wondered who in the world would be coming to our home on such a cold raw day. Mother came to my bedroom door and said, "Jane, there is someone here to see you. He's an officer from the service." She helped me up from the bed, leading me into the living room. Standing there with a letter in his hand was an army Chaplin.

"Mrs. Turnor," he began. I could hear him saying Sgt. Turnor was missing somewhere in Germany, but I kept thinking, "Why can't I get it straight? What is he talking about?"

The room started spinning and spinning. "I don't feel very well," I said to Mother. "I'm so dizzy." And then there was total darkness. "Where am I," I remembered thinking. It's so dark. That's the last thought I had until I heard Daddy saying, "Jane, Jane, Jane, dear. Wake up. Your baby boy is hungry."

My baby boy? What is he saying? What was that sound? I could hear a baby crying but from where? Suddenly I remembered. Trevor's missing, but what was that sound?

Someone was crying from somewhere. Oh, God. It's a baby. I could barely open my eyes.

Then it all came back to me. The room had spun around and around. I must have fainted. "Take it easy, Jane," Dad was saying. "You have a fine baby boy. Now let's get him some supper."

Mother helped me with my gown and I helped Trevor, Jr. to start nursing. Soon he was sound asleep. While he was nursing, I checked him over from head to toe. How precious were those cute little fingers and toes. His tiny ears were just like Trevor's, I remember laughing.

I couldn't believe all this had happened while I was completely out. Mother said my water broke immediately after I fainted. Dad had called our old Dr. Roberts. He came as quickly as he could. Trevor, Jr. was born within an hour. There were no complications for me or the baby.

I learned later that the chaplin stayed until the doctor assured him I was going to be alright. I've often wondered how he must have felt. I'm sure he had lots of experiences but none quite like the day little Trevor was born.

I cried a little then, watching this first baby of ours sleep. What if Trevor never got to see him? What if he never came home again? Dad could sense what I was feeling. "Jane," Dad said. Funny that I can recall his exact words after all these years. "You just have to keep believing Trevor will be okay. There were lots of men missing from our company in the last war. But a lot of them were found. Trevor is smart. He'll figure out a way to get back if that is what has happened. You just have to have faith that he is alive and will survive."

"Right now you have someone else to think about." Daddy's and Mother's advice had always been right for the occasion. So why should it be any different now? I had to think of this new little one in my arms. I also had to think of Trevor's parents.

They came the next morning. Mr. and Mrs. Turnor were firm believers that there was hope for Trevor. They had a faith that could move mountains, but I saw a tear form and fall from each one when they held their first grandson for the very first time.

"Everything's goin' to be alright, Miss Jane," Trevor's mom said, with his dad nodding agreement and saying, "I ope to tell you hit will be alright, Darlin'."

This only made them stronger in my eyes. Now, I knew they were just like the rest of us. They would never give up hope for Trevor's safety and return.

When anyone was sick at our house, they were brought into the living room until they were well for as long as I could remember. That's how it was with me. The next morning after Trevor was born, my parents moved my bed into the living room and placed Trevor's bed there too—beside me—bringing it down from upstairs. Back then you had to stay in bed for over a week after the birth of a child, but that's no longer true, thank goodness. I can remember being so weak once I was allowed to get up.

Mother would say, "No one's going to stay in an old cold bedroom away from the rest of the family if I can help it." There you could see what was happening around you and you didn't feel isolated. The fireplace was always burning in cold months, and it was cozy and warm. A big log was brought in, taking two persons to heave it into the fireplace where it would burn for hours and hours.

There were other things about those days while confined I remember now, just as if they had happened not so long ago.

At least three times a week, a churn was set by the fireplace, covered with a white cloth. In the churn was mostly cream skimmed off the top of milk. The heat from the fire clabbered the cream, and when Mother found an hour or so, she churned the contents with the dasher—up and down, up and down while sitting in one of the big rockers, until butter began to form. She would then lift it out, take it to the kitchen, shaping it together while running cool water through the soft, squishy form to take out any milk left in the butter.

Sometimes she used her round wooden mold with a flower design cut into the center or shaped it into a rectangle, placing the butter into the container, leaving it for a few minutes, then turning it over, bringing out a beautiful design imprinted on the butter. She often put these shapes into a glass covered butter dish, some round, some oblong, setting it in the old ice box or on the kitchen table.

How many times had I seen her perform this ritual I couldn't begin to count. All I know is it tasted wonderful. We never knew about calories then. I hadn't thought about making butter in a long time. Funny how we move on to other things in our lives, but those moments with Mother churning I'll treasure forever.

While thinking about being confined to the bed after little Trevor's birth, something else stands out in my memory concerning our Living Room from this old house when I was almost thirteen years old; something I hadn't thought about in a long time.

I mentioned before about our fireplace and how most of the time a big fire was kept going to help keep the house warm in the winter months. Since there was no screen in front of it, we knew not to get too near, but this particular morning my brother and I weren't remembering what we'd been taught.

It was Saturday, a week before Christmas. The evening before Daddy had taken all of us to the company Christmas party in the basement of a church in town. His company had presents and a big bag of goodies for all the kids.

This bag of goodies held chocolate covered cherries, hard Christmas candy, bubble gum, and a bag of popcorn, one apple, an orange, and to top all of that, the little girls were given a baby doll, and being almost thirteen, I received a bottle of perfume which smelled just like apple blossoms.

The boys also received a bag of goodies, and their present was a Big Little Book. This was another one to add to Luke's collection, which he kept on his bookcase in his room upstairs.

The next morning being Saturday, Daddy was home and he and Mother were having breakfast while Luke and I were in the living room, still excited about the Christmas party the previous evening.

Our cousin, the same age as Luke, dropped by to see us and we showed him our gifts from the evening before. We shared some of our candy, got out the popcorn, and started playing to see who could catch a handful of popped corn by throwing it up and catching it in our mouths. We three took turns in front of the fireplace.

I was still dressed in my long robe and gown, keeping up pretty good with the boys, I thought. I threw one up, catching it, sitting back down in one of the big rockers.

My cousin sat over from me, when he excitingly said, "Jane, your robe is on fire!" I looked down and the blaze was coming up around where I was sitting. It scared me so badly that I started running toward the kitchen.

Now Luke and I were not always angels to one another, and it was not unusual for us to disagree, but Daddy knew by my screams something had happened that somehow didn't involve Luke and me in a normal quarrel, he told me later.

He jumped up from the table, ran to the doorway that went into the living room, and I ran right into his arms. He grabbed my robe, tearing it from around me where it had been stitched together in an empire waistline pattern. While tearing it off, he burned his hands, and also the backs of my legs were slightly burned. We both were treated with an old burn salve to ease the stinging which Mother had.

I've often wondered if this had happened while I was alone, what would I have done. At that time, I didn't know to get down and roll to stop the flames. Thank goodness Daddy was there that morning! It has been a long time since that Saturday, and I thank my lucky stars for him, then and now.

I wasn't burned too badly, for I got my first perm that day. My good friend, Opal, our neighbor, who said the preacher had prayed for me the time I was so sick on the front porch, went to town with us, staying with me while Mother did some shopping. If I'm not mistaken, my mother paid $9.00 for my perm that day. I still remember being so proud of my long curly hair. I've had lots of perms, but never have I experienced anything like the day I got my first perm.

When spring came, I moved back to my bedroom with my baby. Trevor, Jr. was a good baby, and it wasn't long before that dimpled cheek began to show just like his Dad's. From his cowlick to his toes, he was Trevor made over.

I can remember laying in the dark thinking about Trevor. Trevor's son, a part of me, was laying there in the same room. Tears would fill my eyes and there were many times I wondered if Trevor would ever get to see his son. But I kept those fears to myself, not wanting Mother and Daddy to lose hope of Luke's return too. I'm sure they had the same thoughts, but kept them hidden as well as they could from me.

It was beginning spring, a new beginning—I kept thinking with hope in my heart, my husband was safe and we would soon hear some good news.

I knew I could go to church, light a candle, and cry, but I wasn't going to do that. The light of hope was in my heart and eyes for Trevor and this new little one.

My grandmother told me one day, "Trevor would be mighty proud of you, Jane, and I am too. Just think, the Lord has let me live long enough to see my great grandson. I never dreamed I would live so long, Darlin' Jane."

I kept busy with our little new one, trying to eat right and drinking lots of milk. The time went by fast, and yet it seemed to drag—I still wrote Trevor as if nothing had happened, telling him about little Trevor, suggesting that it might be simpler to call him Trev. So Trev was his name from then on.

Six weeks later from the time of Trev's birth, I received a message that his Daddy was safe and no longer missing. And that's when I cried for sure. We all were so happy to get such wonderful news, including his parents. His Dad and his English-Irish pronunciation, with a very deep brogue and accent kept saying over and over, "Our prayr's have been answered. Our prayr's have been answered. Hit's a miracle, Jane. Hit's a miracle."

After the war was over, he told us how he was able somehow to get through enemy lines finding his way back to another American company. Some good German farmers had helped him survive by giving him hard bread and milk. He drew a map from their directions, traveling mostly at night—hiding and sleeping during the day.

Still thinking about Trevor and his ordeal, I slipped into my bedroom in my memories and thoughts.

<u>My Bedroom</u>

The bedrooms and kitchen were wallpapered, just like the living room, only different patterns. I loved my bedroom which had two windows. One opened onto the porch, and the other opened to the west part of the yard. My bed was a small iron one painted white. Sometimes Mother would paint it a different color, but she always came back to white.

The top of the bed was rounded and high, and the bottom the same way but low. I had a night stand that stood by my bed, always a book laid there along with my Bible. A dresser Mom had inherited from somewhere set in my room with a beautiful beveled mirror hanging above it.

Also in my bedroom was a fireplace used only if it was terribly cold or if I needed to study alone in the room. A mantel set above the fireplace. It held some really old pictures of my great grandfathers and great uncles and aunts. Sometimes I'd look at them and wonder just what had happened in their lives. Their clothes were really strange to me. They all looked so solemn and erect when the camera was snapped.

"I named you right when I named you, Jane," Daddy said more than once. "You are the spittin' image of my oldest sister. She was tall and her hair was black as coal, just like you."

I used to wonder while looking at Aunt Jane's picture with that huge head of hair if she ever had headaches, or if she had big feet like I had. But I never did ask Daddy. I never wanted to hurt his feelings, for he always made it sound like a compliment.

I never really knew what happened to Aunt Jane, but I think she fell in love with a "no good" and he broke her heart—at least that's what I heard growing up. But how do you die from a broken heart? I used to wonder. Then I learned that Aunt Jane moped around and didn't really take care of herself after being jilted, took pneumonia, and died. Poor Aunt Jane. What really did happen in her life? Guess we'll never know for sure.

Thinking of my kin folks of long ago, I thought of Memorial Day. Decoration Day, that's what Mother called it. We'd make our yearly trek to the cemetery to decorate the graves. There we'd cut the grass with a small scythe from uncles' and aunts', my great grandparents', and my grandfather's final resting places, most people I never knew except by the pictures in our home. I remember on several occasions taking sandwiches for our lunch on this special day. We'd sit in between the graves on the green grass and eat. Somehow it made you feel as if you were a part of them, not just pictures on a mantel.

Luke and I often wondered if our kinfolk really knew we were there. "I think they do," I always answered. "Otherwise I wouldn't feel so close to them." I can still see Luke nodding his thick blonde head in agreement, while eating a dill pickle Mother had brought from the pickling barrel.

The roses were in bloom the last of May, just in time to decorate the grave sites. We'd take bunches of them carefully wrapped in newspaper. After the graves were tidied up like they should be, Mother and Grandma would set the roses at the head of each in a blue quart jar. Then we'd leave and walk back home, sometimes in silence.

Only one time did I see Mother and Grandma cry as they stood by Grandpa's grave. "He was such a good man and was hoping you'd be a girl for me," Grandma said to my mother. "Why did he have to leave us so soon?" Then she stopped abruptly. "I have no right to question God," she said, as she turned and dried her tears on her homemade cotton apron held on by little straps over the shoulders with ties in the back around her middle.

But back to my bedroom. There was a chest-of-drawers but no closet, along with the dresser. A make-shift line was strung from one side of a corner to the other. That's where my clothes were hung. When I was nearly sixteen, Dad built me a closet. We all know old houses didn't have closets years ago. A closet was an afterthought seemingly.

Suddenly a smile broke upon my face as I thought about the courage it took for Mother to do what she did one time when I was a young teen.

I had become very lax in keeping my bedroom neat and my bed made. For weeks I had gone off to school not making my bed even though Mother had reminded me several times.

One day during class, about 9:00 a.m., I was summoned to the office. When I got there, the principal said my mother had called, wanting me home immediately. I didn't ask why. I just took off in a run. We lived almost a mile from the junior high school, and I ran all the way, trying to imagine what could have happened.

Running up the pathway, jumping the little creek and the garden gate, while sending the guineas screeching, I was nearly out of breath upon reaching the step. There sat Mother and Grandma, talking like they always did as if nothing had happened.

"What's wrong?" I cried out, fearing the worse thing in the world at that moment.

Looking at me direct, Mother said in a firm but soft voice, "Jane, you forgot to make your bed again this morning."

For a moment, I stood there with my mouth open, I'm sure partly from running and partly from surprise, with lots of questions in my brain, such as realizing the principal knew why Mother had summoned me home and how I would feel when I would have to go to the office to get my return slip to enter classes again. But all he said while passing him in the hall was, "Hi Jane—a beautiful day isn't it?" Also I wondered why she hadn't asked for Luke to come home and make his bed up proper-like, but I wouldn't dare mention my thoughts. Luke just pulled the covers up over his pillows and that took care of his bed making.

"Yes ma'am," I weakly replied to Momma, opening the screen and going inside to do my forgotten chore. I felt a little angry that she had done such a thing but knew it was useless to answer any other way, as I went about making my bed carefully.

Besides all of that, I was embarrassed for Grandma to know what I had been neglecting to do. She never mentioned it, not ever, for I'm sure she knew I had learned a lesson I'd never forget. There are some lessons that stay with you for a lifetime; I can attest to this one.

Still standing almost in the same spot as my bedroom once was, I remembered I'd never forgotten the mile I ran that morning nor have I ever left my bed unmade for any length of time to this day.

What fun it was for a friend or cousin to spend the night. When we were young, we'd sleep on the floor. My bed was a twin size, so we'd have to sleep on the floor, just like my kids would do growing up. We'd talk until the wee hours of the next day, mostly about boys, of course.

Besides the mantel full of pictures, there was one picture I loved. It hung close to my bed. There was a little boy and a little girl crossing an old foot log with part of the boards missing. Right behind them was an angel with her arms out to guide them. To this day, I can see the glow on the face of the angel. Sometimes with the blaze from the fire lapping upward and sending out a small light, I could see the picture as it shone in the dark. It helped me many times to drift off to sleep, unafraid.

Thinking about the angel picture, my thoughts went to the time it became apparent the house and farm were too much for our parents.

"When you're home next time, Jane, we'll divide the furniture and the household furnishings between you and Luke," Mother told me over the phone one day.

On my next trip home, we did their wishes, moving Mother and Daddy to a smaller place. They took only what they needed for their new home, leaving the decisions to us about dividing things.

I told Luke then if I didn't get anything else, I wanted the picture of the angel guiding the children across the broken foot log, for that picture meant so much to me, and he knew the reason why.

"It's yours," he said. "It was always in your room—I think girls study more about angels than boys do anyway."

I had caught a glimmer of sadness in his voice as we both remembered Beulah Belle at that instant—our lovely friend from many years gone by.

When I returned to my home that year, the picture was with me, hanging to this day in our bedroom. When our children asked about my angel picture, I always told them about it hanging in my bedroom when I was growing up and the comfort it gave me on many occasions, always remembering my dearest friend, Beulah Belle, to them.

For a long time I never entered my bedroom that I didn't think of Beulah Belle. Sometimes in teasing her, I called her BB. We were so close, the best of friends. Her burnished red-golden hair hung down past her shoulders in natural curls. It looked as if someone had polished it until it shone, glassy-like. Her skin was creamy-white with her cheeks slightly pink—a picture any artist would have loved to capture.

As I mentioned before, Beulah Belle and I, when we were small, would dress up in our mothers' or grandmothers' clothes, pretending to be traveling on a train while carrying their old pocketbooks and handbags—going from our house to our playhouse down by the beautiful wild roses. The only two places we'd ever heard about were Hot Springs and Cleveland, so that's where we would pretend to go.

As we grew older, we told each other our innermost secrets and desires. Nothing was kept from one another. We spent many nights together, either at her house or mine, laughing and talking until we fell asleep.

Sometimes we talked about angels while looking at my picture up close by my bed. Beulah Belle said she really believed in angels, for her mother had told her one came and stood at the foot of her bed the night Beulah Belle was born. Many times she told me how her mother described the angel that stood there with golden long flowing hair cascading over a beautiful white robe with her arms out—stretched toward her mother.

"Then what happened?" I always asked, for I wanted to know more about this angel Beulah Belle made so special.

"Then I was born," she would reply, "and the angel went away." This always sent a chill down my back every time she mentioned it, which was every time she spent the night with me.

I asked Mother if she saw an angel when Luke and I were born. "No, Jane, I didn't, but I think every mother has an angel when their baby is born."

I'm sure one was with me when our little ones came into the world, even though I was out like a light when Trevor was born.

On any given day in the summer or fall, you could find Beulah Belle and me in the tall millet meadow where it rippled in the wind like rippling waters. The wild daisy, black-eyed Susan, and Queen Ann's Lace grew there along with the grains.

I often thought the wind in the millet reminded me of a huge hand that swept down softly, sending the tall grain heads and their bodies blowing while leaning against one another. Then another wind would come like another hand, lifting them back up where they stood straight and tall once again.

We'd take a quilt, spread it on the green grass, and pick some daisies, making daisy chains for our hair. While constructing circles of flowers, we would try to guess who the other was thinking about. And of course it was always Luke and Trevor. Many a daisy lost her petals from our hands while we said over and over, "He loves me, he loves me not." Somehow, if it was someone you loved, you could always make the petals come out just right.

Beulah Belle was in love with Luke and had been from the time we were small children. Luke liked the attention too, especially after he was fourteen.

"Now, don't you ever tell Luke I love him," she made me promise.

"Cross my heart and hope to die," I always repeated with my arms crossed across my heart.

BB was to spend the night with me when we learned she was awfully sick with the flu. Then we heard the doctor had come and she was moved to the hospital because of pneumonia. In less than a week, Beulah Belle had died.

"It can't be true," I screamed to Mother. "It can't be true," while tears ran down her face and mine. But it was true.

She was as lovely in death as in life. Her gown was white with little flecks of red that glistened when the light caught up the flecks that matched her beautiful reddish gold hair. I kept thinking she looked just like the angel in the picture that hung on the wall in my bedroom. Why had I not ever noticed that before so I could have told her.

I couldn't but question why God hadn't sent an angel to help Beulah Belle live like he had the night she was born. It was right after the funeral when I told Mother this, and she replied, "You don't question God, Jane," a statement from Mother that has stayed with me from that day on, the same statement Grandma had used at the cemetery.

That winter several of our neighbors died from the flu. Mother was very protective of Luke and me, but no one in our family ever got the flu. I remember when we were kids, at the first signs of a cold, she would get out an old piece of flannel, dob it real good with Vicks salve, pin it to our undershirt, pull another shirt and sweater over our heads, and off we'd go— smelling to high heavens, I'm sure. Everybody I knew had on one, so guess we got used to the odor emitting from the flannel pieces. At night, a new blob was administered with Mother then holding the flannel up to the fireplace until it was heated real good. She'd place it on to our chests, pinning it once again to our undershirts, before we donned our pajamas. And off to bed we'd go, snug and warm, content and safe in Momma and Daddy's home.

"Where have the years gone?" I asked myself, standing there in what was once my bedroom. I suddenly recalled the event, now, as well as then, for I had never seen Luke act so grown up as he did at Beulah Belle's funeral. He stood with the men around the grave while the preacher gave the benediction. Not a tear fell; I know, because I could see his beautiful brown eyes, and they looked right past me as if he was in a trance.

That evening, now so long ago, I went up to his bedroom where he had gone right after supper. I told him then what I had promised BB I'd never tell him. But it was different now. She was gone and to heaven I was sure.

He was lying on his bed with her school picture there beside him.

With my face all red, my eyes swollen from crying from the loss of my friend, I blurted out, "BB loved you, Luke. She loved you so much. She made me promise I would never tell you. And I promised and hoped I would die. But now I don't care if I die or not. If I do, then I would be with her. I just thought you should know."

"I know Jane," he said softly. "I loved her too. She knew I did. I held hands with her one time. She knew I did," he repeated. "I'll never forget her. I might marry someone else someday, but I'll never forget Beulah Belle." With that, tears came to those big brown eyes, and I left him to deal with his sorrow alone.

Luke did marry after the war was over. He married Phoebe, my other dear friend. I know he never forgot Beulah Belle, but he's happy as any man can be with a wonderful wife and a house full of kids.

Beulah Belle was buried in our family cemetery with my Great Grandparents, Caleb and Elizabeth, Grandpa, Aunt Jane, and all the others. I was content to know my family of long ago were there with her. Every year when we came home on vacation there was a single rose in the vase on her grave—I knew who had placed it there.

Her marker held a vase, which was adorned with an angel who had long, flowing hair and outstretched arms, resembling the angel picture I cherish so much.

Even now, with no walls here, I can close my eyes and hear BB's melodious laughter. It was a laughter that has lingered for all these many years. My heart still aches for her. Just like now, her memory is as clear as a bright summer day. Thinking of BB and her short life, I entered Mom and Dad's bedroom.

Mom and Dad's Bedroom

From my bedroom to Mom's and Dad's was across the living room. It was big, but not as big as the living room. Their bed was an iron one too from Grandma's. It had a rounded back with spoke-like pieces that fitted into the top. For a long time, they had a feather bed. Most everyone had a feather bed then. Each morning she would fluff up the mattress and smooth the counterpane down with a broom handle. It was perfectly made up.

When I was about eight years old, I was watching Grandma making up her feather bed at her house.

"Did I ever tell you," she said, "what my friend did to me after I had made up my bed one morning?"

"No," I answered, "what friend?"

"It was Aunt Susan, but everybody called her Aunt Su Su. We were the best of friends," Grandma began, with her face crinkling up. "One morning she came to see me. I had just finished making up my bed and was smoothing it out with the broom handle. Just as I turned away, Aunt Su Su jumped right into the middle of it, crushing it down."

"I was shocked at first, not believing what she had done. Then we both laughed until we cried. Every time I make up this old bed, I always remember Su Su, and all the good times we had together. She's with the angels now," Grandma said reverently and reservedly.

I would like to have known Aunt Su Su. She must have been a lot of fun, I thought. Now, I wish, for just one time, I had jumped into Momma's feather bed and surprised her like Aunt Su Su did Grandma, but I imagine I would have been the one surprised. I smiled at the thought.

Every bed in our house was an iron one except the one in the other bedroom at the top of the stairs on the right. The bed Mother and Daddy slept in was the same one in which I got my start into this world, I'm pretty sure. As I said before, about once a year, Mother would get on a painting spree and paint every iron bed in the house. You would never know what color she would come up with. She did this while we were in school. We'd come home and find our bed a different color. No one in the family seemed to mind. Whatever color she chose to use was alright with us.

A tall dresser with a long mirror on one side and three drawers on the other belonged in Mother and Daddy's bedroom. They had a large cloak cabinet there also. Hers and Daddy's clothes were kept in this. Most people like us didn't own a lot of clothes, and as I said before, there wasn't very much closet space. We had a small closet by the fireplace in the living room to hang our good winter coats, and a clothes rack by the kitchen door for our everyday wear to do our chores in. Also our boots were tossed under the rack when we pulled them off while sitting by the kitchen stove, the "old iron horse," as we called it.

Also in their bedroom were family pictures. A large picture of her Daddy hung there, the Daddy she never got to see. And too there was a picture of Grandma beside of Grandpa. On the east wall hung a portrait of Mother and Daddy taken while he was still in uniform just as World War I ended. They were both looking toward the left with Daddy just a little behind Momma. I asked her one day what she was looking at, and she replied, "The future, I'm sure." Again, I thought if Daddy hadn't returned, I wouldn't be here right now. I thanked my lucky stars that I had been given a chance at life.

Daddy never talked very much about World War I. I think it was too painful for him. When he mentioned Howard, his best friend, who was killed in France, he would get this far-away look in his eyes. Mother then would somehow turn the conversation to another subject. Soon Daddy would join in and be his old self once again.

When I looked into the space that was once Mother and Daddy's bedroom, there it was in my mind's eye as if it was there in reality—her old Singer sewing machine.

As I've said before, Mother never liked to sew or maybe never felt she had time, but as a child, I remember her fitting me with new dresses for school she had made.

There was a story behind the old Singer machine for sure, and it goes like this. Mother was expecting me just any time now, they always said when telling the story.

One day at work, Daddy suddenly had the urge to go home to check on Mother. When he got there, she was just fine; in fact, she was happy as a lark for she had just purchased a new sewing machine. The salesman was still there on the front porch figuring out the payments per month. They had a good laugh when Daddy explained why he had come home so early.

It became quite a joke with all their friends, often asking if the little wife had made him some new clothes with that brand new sewing machine.

Then I remember another time when Mother gave me the Singer, for Trevor and I were moving away to his station while he was still in the Army.

"You take this Jane," she said, pointing to the sewing machine. "I know one day you are going to need it when those little girls start coming along. If I need to sew, I'll just buy me one." And she did, putting it in the same spot the first Singer had been.

Mother was right. I used the sewing machine many times, but now it sets in my living room as an antique. It has a special place in my heart.

I smile now remembering how Daddy took off work one afternoon because he was concerned about Mother and me.

Yes, this was its special nook so many years ago, but now I see where other things were once placed in Mother and Daddy's bedroom as I look and remember.

The little rickety bedside table held the alarm clock, the Bible, and the old oil lamp. I could see Mother before going to bed, taking her oil lamp from room to room making sure everything was in order before she blew out the flame and got in her own bed.

They both were up at 4:30 every morning, getting a good start on their day. They'd punch up the coals and soon have a roaring fire in the fireplace. They would then hurry into the kitchen and build one there in the old cook stove. A big breakfast was a must back then to get you through the morning until lunchtime. While Mother made breakfast, Daddy did some of the chores like slopping the hogs or feeding the horse if it was wintertime.

My Daddy liked to hunt. Like most men then, he owned some kind of a gun. His was a double-barrel shot gun. It was kept under their bed, never loaded. When Luke was 14, he got his first gun. Daddy and Luke tramped the farm over looking for rabbits or squirrels. Many a holiday we ate fried rabbit or squirrel and gravy.

Smiling to myself, I remembered how we never let Daddy forget the night he heard strange noises and went to investigate.

Mother liked sunflowers, having them growing in the garden, and a tall one grew not far from our kitchen door.

That certain night, he got up, removed his gun from under the bed, loaded it, and stepped out the back door cautiously and silently.

He stood by the kitchen listening to the night noises, when he was suddenly made aware (he thought) that someone was standing by him. Slinging his gun to the ground, drawing his fists back to defend himself, he realized it was Mother's tall sunflower.

"You could never guess what I just did," Dad told Mother when he came back to bed laughing. When a fellow can laugh at himself, then you know he's an all-around good guy, and that's how Dad was—able to laugh at himself even though we teased him quite a lot about the old sunflower for a long time.

I never liked guns, but my mother could shoot as well as any man. Once I remember Daddy had to be away on his job. On the nightstand that week sat a box of shells along with the alarm, her Bible, and the old oil lamp. I felt just as secure when Daddy was gone as I did when he was there. My mother had everything under control I was sure. It never crossed my mind otherwise.

43

<u>The Red Carpeted Stairway</u>

Still feeling a kind of contentment before leaving Mother and Daddy's bedroom, I looked up as if to see the stairway leading to the other two bedrooms. These steps I could not trace with my shoe but could only climb them in my memory.

Fifteen steps led to the first landing, and then there were six more before reaching the top. There was a handrail with the newel squared off at the end where a flower pot or an ornament could set. A short handrail was on the upper side of the other steps leading to the top landing.

The boys, my great uncles, being rambunctious, often slid down the longest banister or handrail, knocking over whatever was on the little square at the end. After several times setting something pretty there, Grandmother Elizabeth gave up the effort, knowing it was useless to keep trying with a houseful of boys.

My Mother, to my knowledge, never set anything on the newel. She must have known Luke and I would slide down every chance we got to the bottom while chasing one another. I'm sure she had heard about her uncles sliding down the rail many years ago from Grandma.

As long as I can remember, a red, slightly worn carpet covered the stairway. Grandfather Caleb had purchased it for the love of his life, Elizabeth. It had outlasted three generations, still bright and colorful when I was young. Besides being on the stairs, it was on the floor connecting the two upstairs bedrooms.

For several years, Grandma told me her family saved their discarded woolen garments, packaging and sending them to a company to be made into carpet. That's how households were able to acquire a carpet in Grandma's time without the cost being too great.

The company which wove the material would then dye the color requested, and Great Grandfather Caleb had requested red because Grandmother Elizabeth had asked that it be red.

Grandma remembered the day the carpet came by train. She and one of her sisters were allowed to go with their father to pick it up. It was wrapped in heavy brown paper with only a speck of red showing at the end. She said they chattered all the way home, being so excited, wishing the old horse and buggy could go a little faster.

"I thought we would never get home for we had to make two stops. One was for Pa to talk to a friend and the other to pick up the newspaper and magazines he loved to read," Grandma said.

"As we turned the corner of the yard, the girls ran to meet us, but the boys didn't. I guess they knew they had a big job awaiting them for they didn't show their excitement like we girls did."

"We couldn't do anything about the carpet until after dinner. Mother sensed we would be hungry after our trip to town, so we ate upon arriving home that afternoon."

Grandma had said it was somewhat of a ceremony when the carpet was laid. "We had never seen anything quite like it when it was unfurled from the top to the bottom step. As soon as dinner was over, the boys and Pa worked until late to lay the carpet. We girls and Mother stood at the bottom step watching and waiting while each step was covered and clamped into place. Finally it was laid and by then it was bedtime."

"We were so excited, sleep was hard to come by for we kept going to the doorway, looking at it again and again. It was about the fanciest thing any of us had ever seen."

Grandma liked to tell about the "carpet party," as she called it, remembering every detail. She began by saying, "My mother, being the kind of person she was, held an afternoon tea for all the ladies in the community to come see the new carpet."

Grandma and her sisters helped with the tea, baking big sugar cookies and little sweet cakes with raisins. It was a grand time, you can well imagine, for all the ladies oohed and awed as they touched and felt, walking up and down the stairway time and time again, exclaiming and marveling over the beauty of it.

"It made Pa happy just to know he had made us happy, including Mother," I remember Grandma saying.

I looked up once again as if I could see what Grandma had told me about the carpet being bought and installed by her father and brothers. What a wonderful time that must have been for the whole family. How beautiful and simple everything seemed to be back then, and yet it seems to me there were problems just like in today's world—only not so many.

Comparing the problems of yesterday with problems of today, I found myself near Luke's bedroom.

Luke's Bedroom

I walked a bit farther, looked up again, realizing I was seeing in my thoughts the room that had belonged to the girls in Grandmother's family. I could just imagine the peals of laughter ringing in this room from Grandma and the others when they were young, a room that had witnessed three births and in later years becoming Luke's, now just a memory, but a pleasant one.

Besides having an iron double bed, Luke had a bookcase that matched his dresser. There were shelves and drawers which were left open much of the time with his socks hanging out. The drawers had little white knobs. They showed up really well since the furniture was black. A big square board was attached to his bookcase; when let down it became a desk. Only a window shade covered his window. The floor there too was covered with linoleum. The room was warm in the winter from the heat going up, but hot in the summer when the air didn't move much. Sometimes a cross breeze from the other bedroom window brought relief to a sweltering body.

I can still hear his feet hitting the floor when Daddy called him to "rise and shine like the sun." He liked his name, Luke Sheldon, named after our grandfather. Luke said his name sounded dignified and important. Daddy, being down to earth, would often say, "If it does that for you, you'd better live up to it, son. I'm sure your grandfather was dignified and important to a lot of people."

"Yes sir, I will," Luke always replied.

Mother kept his room spick and span while he was off fighting the war. I knew she went there to pray for his safety and well being every day all the many months he was gone. There are some things you just know, somehow.

How well I remember my brother wanting a paper route for some time when Daddy finally agreed, making sure Luke understood his duties with a job and his duties at home.

In the winter months, the paper was delivered on Sunday only, but in the summer when school was out, it was every day, from June first to September first. Those delivered on Sunday would have to be picked up by 6:00 a.m. He set his alarm clock to ring early, and off he'd go to get his bundle of papers.

Sometimes he'd have to walk over a mile, pick up the papers, carrying them in a big container, delivering them walking to each home which was two miles or more. This was in the winter months, Sunday only, when he couldn't ride his bicycle because of snow and ice.

It was different with the summer delivery, for he could ride his bike, picking up his papers and taking them to each home of the subscribers.

Many times I delivered the papers with him, but only in the summer months. We became acquainted with several new people, also getting reacquainted with our old friends and neighbors.

On one of these delivery trips, our really old friend showed us how he made apple cider, afterwards giving us a vinegar jug full to take home to Mother. We made many friends from delivering papers—friends we'll remember forever.

Even now it seems I can smell the aroma from the many piles of apples he had stacked up all around while he placed several at a time into a cider press. Never have I seen as many honey bees in my life while they hovered over the stacked piles of apples in a continual buzz and hum, seeking out the sweet juice.

This he only did in his spare time, for his main job was to shoe horses. How fascinating it was for us to watch a horse getting shod while it stood perfectly still while he attached the shoes to the horse's feet. Maybe this is the reason I've always loved the poem, "The Village Blacksmith," for it brings back lovely remembrances of my childhood.

Besides being ambitious, Luke was well liked by the girls. His eyes were brown and his hair blonde—a perfect combination. He had lots of lasting friendships with his fellow companions. He was always a good brother to me. We would have done anything for one another, and still do. With this thought in mind, I moved from where Luke's bedroom had been in my memories to the other bedroom upstairs.

<u>The Other Bedroom</u>

While telling the story of the red carpeted stairway, I mentioned the two bedrooms upstairs. The bedroom Luke slept in was the one he was born in, like Mother and I. The other was used only when company came, for this bedroom had a significance about it that was somehow sacred.

The "Other Room," the name we gave it, was on the right of the stairway, across from Luke's bedroom. This room was originally the bedroom for my great uncles while growing up in the old house. By the time Great Grandmother Elizabeth became ill, the sons had all left home and she began to occupy the other room at the top of the stairs. Perhaps she felt a closeness to her sons by being there, remembering each one, especially the one who she knew in her heart would never be home again.

My grandma, while she was still able to climb the stairs, kept the room spotless and in the same time period her mother, Elizabeth, had lived. When Grandma no longer could keep it the way she thought it should be kept, she passed the keeping of it on to Mother.

When I was young, being sometimes curious, I would slip up the stairs, enter the room, and look around at the beauty of it to my childish eyes.

Somehow I knew this is where my Great Grandmother Elizabeth had died. At that time, I didn't know she had died from breast cancer and a hemorrhage of the brain. People didn't talk about things and illnesses like they do now. As I grew older, I caught conversations from Mother and Grandma about Great Grandmother Elizabeth's death.

The bed in the room with its tall headboard took a large section of the room itself, reaching nearly to the ceiling. It had belonged to my great grandparents, bought when they first married.   The top was rounded into a scroll-like shape, embellished with carvings that resembled wheat with spirals of grain, reaching out upon the headboard. In the center of this headpiece was an oval mirror with tiny wheat stacks carved all around the beveled edge.

A huge bolster pillow lay stretched across the top with the embroidered counterpane which showed a huge blue basket with flowers of all kinds and colors spread upon the bed—reaching about three-fourths down before the dust ruffle took the remaining space, nearly touching the floor itself.

A big square steamer trunk set at the foot of this enormous bed. In the springtime or whenever she thought about it, Mother would open the windows to let the room air out. Inside of this trunk were their love letters written especially while Great Grandfather Caleb was a prisoner of war in Virginia, Georgia, South Carolina, and North Carolina from 1863 to 1865. They were bound in a leather container tied loosely with a leather string.

He always began with this salutation to my great grandmother, "My Dear Elizabeth."

Not once did he complain about being a prisoner. He was more interested in what everyone at his home and neighborhood were doing, whether they were going to church during the revival or if some of his friends had gotten married.

Beside the bed was a big square table with fancy carved work on the legs. I'm sure it had been purchased the same time as the bed, for the same designs were on the top of it. A large embroidered square scarf with the same pattern as the counterpane, or spread, as we now say, was lovingly placed upon the table with the points hanging down on all four sides.

This table held Elizabeth's Bible and an oil lamp with a globe that had "Home Sweet Home" painted on it. Also upon the table sat a picture of my great grandparents on their wedding day.

Her dress was white with a squared lace collar which hung full over the shoulders, with tiny seed buttons and tucks down the front. You could tell her hair was twisted into a bun at the nape of her neck.

He wore his Union army uniform with his sword at his side and his government pin in his lapel, the same pin that went to the grave with him.

She was quite pretty and he so handsome with a full beard.

This picture had been taken from an old tin type, my mother told me while I was still in my teens. We often looked at this picture, and Momma would say, "Oh, how I miss my grandfather. He was like a father to me since I never knew my dad."

The biggest rocking chair I've ever seen sat in this room, facing the bed, the same rocker Luke and I sat on while Mother read to us when we were still young. Mother decided to use the rocker from there after Daddy came home with one for himself. They were both placed in front of the fireplace, and they used them most every day after that. It was made of oak with a red leather seat and back with gold colored upholstery tacks driven in by someone who was very adept at his trade.

As I got older, I tried to visualize my grandmother as a baby being rocked in this big chair. I'm sure she cried like other babies, but I had never seen her cry but one time, and then only for a minute.

Since this room was used only when company came, perhaps I would have kept it just like Grandma and Mother had, had I not moved away; that is, if Mother and Daddy had wanted me to have the old home place.

Imagining and remembering how it once was, I moved from the "Other Room" into the kitchen in my thoughts.

The Kitchen

While I was growing up, this room was my favorite place in the old house, as my thoughts began to return while walking off the limit where the kitchen used to be. How many people had come through this place, sat at that big old table, laughed and talked while enjoying their meal, no one would ever know for sure. But Grandma liked to remember some of the happenings in here that held a special place in her heart.

She was full of stories about her big family of brothers and sisters. They played pranks on one another occasionally if it meant getting a laugh or two, and this is one of them.

The story goes that the preacher took turns going home with the parishioners after church. It was my great grandparents' time to feed the pastor on this certain Sunday, and they went all out to have a fine dinner for him and his wife.

My grandmother had a delicious cake recipe she used for the Sunday dinner. I'm sure it was her famous nine egg pound cake. In order for it to cool, she placed it on top of the tall china cabinet in the kitchen, out of reach of the boys, she thought.

While my grandmother was busy with other things, one of the older boys slipped in, dug out the inside of the cake underneath as much as he could without it being noticed, and set it back upon the top of the tall cupboard. He and his brothers then had themselves a little cake feast and a big laugh.

Come Sunday after church, a big dinner was prepared and eaten with Great Grandpa sitting at the head of the table doing much of the talking as usual.

After the main meal was over, since Grandma had baked the cake, she was the one who got to serve it. She reached up on the cupboard, got it down, and prepared to slice it, when much to everyone's surprise, and especially Grandma's, the cake fell in—in fact, it collapsed. She immediately knew who the culprits were, her brothers.

"At first I didn't know what to do, then I wanted to be angry, but I couldn't let the preacher see that I had a temper so I just started laughing, joined in by all around that big old oval table, while the boys pointed fingers at one another, for they all had a share in the mischief. They teased me unrelentingly for months."

"Well," Grandma went on by saying, "the preacher got hisself a message out of that incident about my cake. That evening at church he reminded everyone no matter how you look on the outside, it's the inside that counts the most."

I can remember how Grandma reminisced about her brothers who went off to war while they were still quite young.

"The years flew by," Grandma would say, "when one day we found ourselves in a war with Spain. Four of my brothers joined up, for they believed if their country was at war then duty demanded they be behind their country."

So off they went, one after the other. The oldest brother (who had tunneled the cake) came to his mother, Elizabeth, in the kitchen, informing her he was joining the army, wishing to tell her goodbye gently. She would not accept what he was trying to tell her, so he ran out from the room up the driveway into the woods. She begged and pleaded, running after him a long distance trying to persuade him not to go. He sat down some distance from her as if he was trying to decide what he should do. He then got up and waved at his mother, disappearing among the trees.

She had stopped, with her tears flowing, giving him a farewell wave, turning going back to the house with a prayer on her lips and hope in her heart that he might be safely returned home one day. But that was not to be.

Elizabeth nor Caleb ever saw him again, for when the war was over, he was discharged in San Francisco, where he met two of his brothers, telling them he would be home in a week or more. He never returned home, was never seen again by his kin. Grandma did receive a letter from him from San Francisco saying he was anxious to get home to see everyone, especially his brothers and sisters and most anxious to catch up on all the news.

No one in the family knew exactly what happened to their son and brother. Detectives were hired, but no answer to his whereabouts was ever found. It was surmised he was probably killed for his mustering-out pay. "He was tall and handsome," Grandma said, "with the bluest of eyes you've ever seen and blonde curly hair."

"Oh what sadness it was when we learned of another dear brother's death," Grandma lamented.

"It seemed we were engulfed with sadness for the longest. He didn't die from bullets in a far away country, but from a dreaded disease. I wondered how I could stand any more, and there again were Pa and Mother Elizabeth to think about."

One of the four brothers died from malaria on board ship coming back to the United States. He was brought home and buried in our family cemetery as his mother and father would be years later. Great Grandmother Elizabeth, while visiting his grave, was heard to say, "At least I know where this son is," referring to the son who never came home from San Francisco.

Another older brother settled in Texas after being discharged from the Army, married, and never came home again for forty years. One day when at last he came home for a visit, he was sitting on the front porch, looking out upon the fields, and he remarked that things were beginning to look as he had remembered them from bygone days.

"You know, Sister," he said to my grandmother, "I should have come back years before, but I couldn't face all the changes with Pa and Ma gone along with my brothers and sisters. I was trying to hold on to a past—a past that I couldn't give up or come back to either. But now I'm here, and it's wonderful to be home and see everyone once again."

A reunion was held on these very grounds for my great uncle—an uncle I had never seen before and would never see again once he returned to his home. The whole community came to make him welcome and to wish him well. It was a great time in our lives, and I'll never forget at the age of 15 meeting my great uncle for the first time, because he had been gone from our family 40 years. My mother was barely five years old when he went off to war, and it was quite a reunion for all of us. He had married and had two children but all had died several years before.

As the war came to a close, the youngest brother made it through safely, coming back to marry his beloved, raising a big family as his Pa and Ma had done. And then World War II came. A son was sacrificed almost in the same place where his father had fought forty some years before.

"Life goes on," Grandma had said. "You live one day at a time—not yesterday, not tomorrow, but only today."

Thinking about my great uncles, I can recall there was one other brother in Grandma's family who did not go off to war but stayed home to help his father on the farm, and in later years he helped others when needed.

My grandmother asked him to plant peach trees in a plot that never had anything like fruit trees growing in it even before she grew up. He asked Luke and me to be his helpers.

We carried water in buckets from the well to be put in each hole where he planted a tree before an early spring that year. We worked right along with him until the job was done. He gave each of us a nickel for being such good workers. That was a big amount to our eyes during the Depression, you can be sure.

Those trees took off growing, and it wasn't long before they were producing wonderfully tasting peaches.

We had all we could eat, and Mother canned several half gallon jars of the fruit. We also supplied the market and the neighbors that particular year sometime in the 1930s. Each year they produced more it seemed.

I remember during a hot August picking peaches while getting the fuzz all over me, but it was still fun, especially to know you had helped start a real orchard and now being able to pick the fruit while enjoying it too.

After recounting the tragedies in her life, Grandmother continued talking to her young listener. I was all ears when she had something to say, knowing how easy it is now to recall the slightest detail.

She began by saying, "All my life, Jane, there hasn't been time for tears, but I believe you've made up for it," she laughed and winked at me.

"You see, when Mother Elizabeth died, your great aunt Ann was barely ten years old. Being the baby in the family, we all loved her so very much. I held her hand at the funeral while also holding back the tears, which would have coursed down my face if I had let them."

"I suppose," she went on to say, "since I was the oldest, little Ann relied on me. Not wanting to disappoint her in any way, I kept the tears to myself while she tried to understand what had taken place with our mother."

"It was the same when your grandfather, great grandfather, Mother Elizabeth, Otis, and dear Sister dying suddenly. I had to blink back the tears for there was always someone else I had to consider. It's not that I don't have tears—they are there for sure—and heavy on the heart," she added.

"But let me tell you now something cheerful," she began. "When your great aunt Ann was six months old, Mother, and Pa went to visit Ma's parents in Missouri. Our mother needed to see her parents, who she hadn't seen for many years. Of course they had to take Ann with them. They were gone six weeks, and how we missed them, especially baby Ann. Ma and Pa left me in charge since I was the eldest. I was a little frightened by my enormous duties but determined to carry them out for they were depending on me."

"We received a letter letting us know the day of their returning, and one of the brothers was to pick them up at the train station. We were so excited of their homecoming and kept vigilance at the window all morning so we'd know when the buggy came in to view."

"Suddenly there it was, with the horse rounding the bend on the turn. We stopped our watch, running out to meet the buggy with each one of us trying to be the first to hold 'Little Ann.'"

"What a homecoming," Grandma stated. "And what a surprise to see our dear little grandmother for the very first time. She had moved away before any of us had been born, including me, the oldest. She had really long hair and I got to help her wash it, which wasn't an easy task; also to comb and braid it, wrapping those braids around her head twice. Our grandmother was so tiny compared to us, always wearing dark clothes with several slips under her long black skirts."

"We enjoyed her visit so much, asking her about Missouri and if she missed her first home. She said she did but was quite happy in her surroundings and would plan to stay there for the rest of her life. And Jane, it was so sad when she had to leave for we knew that in all probability we would never see her again."

Grandma continued by saying, "Little Ann had grown so much and we were all so happy to have her back home again. I reckon we spoiled her a bunch when she was young, but she was always right there to help the rest of us—and she was there when Otis and your mother were born, staying with me until I was able to care for my family once again. She was and still is a devoted sister."

These stories, some sad, some with happy endings, still tear at my heart strings even now as I walk off this room as it had been so many years ago.

Yes, this was my favorite room in this wonderful old house, but now other thoughts had entered my head for I suddenly remembered an evening of long ago which involved our family.

Many a problem was solved here around the old kitchen table, from an algebra problem to an almost ruined life.

Luke was sixteen when he was accused by a girl in the community of getting her pregnant.

Just about supper time one evening, I was still sitting out in the swing embroidering. Mother had already announced supper would be ready in five minutes. Everyone was to be ready to eat when she got it on the table.

We were having revival meetings again that week. In fact, it had gone on over two weeks. Mother was hurrying to get supper over so we could attend. Mother enjoyed the singing as well as the visiting preacher, seeing old friends and catching up on all the news around.

She didn't get to see many in the community unless she went to the ladies aid, which met once a month. They met in the church in the fall and winter months. They didn't meet in summer as there were too many other things to do such as gardening, canning, and pickling, along with other duties.

Mother most always went to the aid, for she would help prepare the luncheon for the others. As I stated before, she didn't care too much about sewing (except to crochet), but she could really prepare a meal that was delicious.

Those ladies turned out beautiful quilts, some of which I can remember were called the Texas Star, the Flower Girl, or the Old Rail Fence. These were sold, giving the money to the church to be used for whatever the need was at the time. Besides the sewing, they just enjoyed being together, so it was a treat to meet at the church and get some visiting in before the evening service started during a revival.

I looked up from my embroidery work that evening to see why the guineas were screeching when I saw our neighbor, Mr. Truc (who by the way no one cared too much about) approaching our front yard. He opened the wooden gate that was attached to the white palings that circled like a fortress all around the yard. There were three gates that served us back then—the front gate, the back gate, and the one leading to Mother's garden—close to where the wild roses grew. These gates served as a barrier to wandering chickens or a larger animal.

"Good evening, Miss Jane," he announced his arrival in a syrupy kind of address. "I would like to speak with your father if you so please," he said as he unhitched the latch to the gate that led to our front yard.

"Yes sir!" I replied, dropping my stitches as well as my embroidery work onto the swing. "I'll get him for you, sir."

"Thank you very much, Miss Jane," still in his syrupy speech.

I hurried into the parlor and on into the living room, where Dad was sitting in his rocker reading the paper awaiting supper. It had been a hot day. Dad and Luke had worked hard in the boiling sun plowing and planting for the new crops.

"Dad," I said as I approached him, "Mr. True wishes to speak with you."

"Mr. True?" Dad asked puzzled.

"Yes sir!" I replied, feeling a foreboding to come.

Dad went lumbering quietly out while I followed a little way—almost into the parlor. He turned to me and said, "Jane, you'd better go tell your mother to hold supper for a few more minutes."

I did as I was told, but supper was held for a long time that evening. We didn't get to eat until way after dark. Even then, no one had much of an appetite, and you can be certain there was no church that evening for us.

I can still see Luke sitting at the table talking to Mother, telling her of the day's events. It had been a good year for crops. He was happy to think that there would be a bountiful yield by August. That meant he could sell part of the gain and make himself some spending money.

"What was all the commotion from the guineas?" Mother asked as I entered the kitchen.

"Mr. True wanted to speak to Dad," I chipped in with my news.

"Whatever for?" Mother looked at me with a question on her countenance as well as her lips.

"I don't know," I said, shrugging my shoulders, "but Dad wants you to hold up supper for awhile."

Mother looked exasperated but relented, putting the prepared food back into pots and some into the warming oven.

I looked at Luke and asked when he had seen Trudy. "Last night," he replied, looking at me quizzically. "I walked her home like I always do. Why?"

"No reason. I just wondered when you'd seen Trudy," I said, filling the water glasses, and giving him the once over.

In just a few minutes we heard a raised voice coming from the front. It was Mr. True. We also heard the names Trudy and Luke. We looked at one another, wondering what in the world was happening.

Not long afterward, Dad came into the kitchen, looking a bit haggard.

"What's wrong, John!" Mother asked. "What did that man want?" She never said Mr. True, for she had no respect for him.

"I'll tell you later Mona." That was my Mother's name. "You and Jane go to the bedroom while I talk to Luke." Dad hardly ever called Mother, Mona. It was always darlin' or sweetheart. I knew right then for sure something serious was happening in our little family. I looked at Luke and saw him swallowing real fast and hard.

Luke looked at Dad with a surprised, questioning look on his face, trying to figure out what was going on.

When we got to the bedroom, we could hear part of the conversation, and it went a little like this.

"I didn't do it, Dad. I walked her home. That's all. That's the truth Dad," I heard my brother say, pleadingly.

Mother and I shivered and cried in her bedroom. She found a handkerchief and began wiping her face furiously. I could tell she was very concerned, besides being mad as a hornet. I'm sure she could have taken Mr. True down a notch or two at that instant. But here she was in her bedroom with her daughter, while her son was pleading with his father for understanding.

Mother whispered to me, "When did Luke go to Daniel McRail's birthday party?"

Last month I remembered and whispered back to her. I also remembered I hadn't been invited—just Luke. I was a little hurt I hadn't gotten an invitation, but after all, they were two years older than I was. I got over it when Mother said I could invite someone to spend the night with me. I invited Phoebe, someone else who liked Luke an awful lot. I remembered every detail of that evening when I was answering Mother in a whisper as well as now.

Luke was promptly in at ten o' clock, his curfew. We heard him come in, talking awhile to Mom and Dad, then going into the kitchen. We came out of my bedroom and followed him into the kitchen ourselves. That's when Phoebe and I talked to him about the party. He told us while we three drank a glass of milk how much fun he had at Daniel's house that evening.

"Did you play kissin' games?" I asked.

Luke looked a little embarrassed, but he answered that they had.

"I'll bet you kissed Trudy," I said accusingly.

"Maybe so," he answered, not looking at Phoebe or me while he tried to give us the silent treatment.

Finally he said, "Why aren't you two asleep already? Tomorrow is Sunday and you'll probably fall asleep in church," he added.

"It will probably be you falling to sleep," I answered. "You won't hear a thing the preacher is saying. You'll be dreaming about Trudy True for sure," making it sound sinful and wicked.

"Maybe so," he answered again just like he had said before, heaving a sigh, looking around, trying to act unconcerned. Suddenly his eyes came to rest on Phoebe as if it was the first time he'd ever seen her, and then he asked how old she was.

"I'm almost fifteen—will be next month."

"I thought you were nearly sixteen," Luke said.

"Really?" Phoebe answered, her eyes sparkling.

Luke then said another nice thing to Phoebe. "Phoebe, from now on I'm going to call you Fe Fe."

"You are? I like that," she beamed. "No one has ever called me that before. It's like being born all over again. I have a new name, Jane," she giggled, looking shy and sort of embarrassed, but pleased as punch.

Luke put his elbows on the table, holding his face in his hands. He smiled and looked admiringly at Phoebe, for he knew he had struck the right chord.

I thought she would never go to sleep. She just couldn't believe Luke thought she was older than she was. And too, he had given her a special name, she reminded me several times.

She kept saying over and over, "Feel my heart, Jane—just feel my heart. It just won't be still. Oh, Jane, do you suppose Luke is up there thinking about me?"

"I'm sure he is Phoebe, or he wouldn't have given you the new name," I replied, half asleep.

I imagine Luke was thinking about Fe Fe—she was the most beautiful of anyone I'd ever known—with her long black hair that hung in little wisps and curls all over. Her Grecian face that held blue, blue eyes—when you might think they should have been dark to match the hair, and her sweet personality. What a combination. She and Beulah Belle were as different as night and day, each beautiful in her own way, and I loved both of them so much and still do.

The next morning she was bubbling over talking to Mother and being so polite and helpful. There was a little smile that played around her lips, a smile that never quite left her face the rest of the day.

From then on, I loved Phoebe like a sister. I prayed nothing would happen to her like what had happened to Beulah Belle and take her away from me.

Still in the kitchen, or rather Mother and I in her bedroom, my thoughts turned back to Luke and his predicament so long ago.

While Mother and I listened for a word to let us know what had taken place, we heard Luke say, "Nothing happened. She's lying—you've got to believe me, Dad. We were with several others. Nothing could have happened," Luke kept saying over and over.

"Since you put it that way, I do believe you son," Dad replied.

I remember that evening clearly now, as if it had just taken place.

Dad and Luke went about their evening chores, such as milking old Claudia, and feeding the hogs. By that time it was nearly dark.

Mother and I went out to the front porch and sat for quite some time. Suddenly she said, "Your dad and Luke will be hungry when they get back in. I need to get their supper on the table."

She got up and went right to the kitchen, heating up the already prepared food.

She had worried enough about the Trues and now it was time to get on with her everyday living and let tomorrow take care of itself. I heard her say this many times (quoting from the Bible), and I'm sure that's what she was thinking that unforgettable evening of long ago.

The very next morning Dad and Luke went to see the girl's father. Sure enough, Trudy had lied. The father laughed and said, with his mossy teeth showing, I'm sure, "I guess Trudy lost her notchin' stick, for she came 'round like she always does, just this mornin', matter of fact."

"It caused us a bit of heartache, Mr. True. Make sure your daughter don't ever accuse my son of doing something he's never done before." We never heard from that family again. They soon moved on to somewhere else, thank goodness.

Trudy was a pretty thing—always laughing and teasing the boys. They hung around her like flies around honey. She was a true blonde with big blue eyes. My brother fell for her like a ton of bricks.

From all of this, he learned a life's lesson, he told me not long afterwards. "All that glitters is not gold—even golden curls."

There were two happy events that happened that day. All was not lost on Mr. True or Trudy. Besides getting the nightmare stopped concerning Luke and Trudy, there was another happening we heard about that same morning.

When Dad and Luke got home, they came into the kitchen from the back porch. Our parents discussed the confrontation with Mr. True and Luke's awakening.

Hardly able to contain himself, Dad then said, "Mona darlin', do I ever have some news for you."

"There's that name again," I thought, as I sat down at the table. "It has to be something unusual like we' ve never heard before, or he wouldn't be calling Mother Mona two days in a row for sure. Yesterday was upsetting enough. Whatever could it be," I questioned in my mind.

"Whatever is it?" Mother asked in a quizzical sort of way.

Dad began to go into the happenings in great detail, with Mother and I listening, forgetting all about the Trues. Dad pushed his coffee cup forward for a refill, while Mother jumped up, filling it, pouring herself another cup.

Dad began: "On the way home from the Trues, we met Mr. Gaston coming down the road in his old Chevy. You know how narrow the road is there on the turn?" he asked, and Mother nodded her affirmation. "Well, we had to pass real slow and cautiously so we stopped to chat awhile. We turned off our machines so we could hear one another."

I thought, "Machines? Nobody ever says "machines" but Grandma. When would they start just saying car or automobile? This kind of old talk was just what it was, old!" But I quickly forgot about it for I was all ears to know about what Mr. Gaston told Dad.

"John," he said, "have you heard what's happened to old Widow Sessions?"

"No! What?" I said, "expecting the very worst."

"Well, John, it appears that she got herself saved last evening at that revival."

"You should have seen Dad," Luke put in his two cents worth with a laugh. "He sat there with his mouth wide open. It was so funny to watch Dad while Mr. Gaston continued talking about Widow Sessions."

"While the congregation was singing "Why Not Tonight," with that new preacher asking for all sinners to come up to the Mourner's Bench, well lo and behold old Widow Sessions walked right up that aisle and gave her hand to the minister. She must have been in the very back pew of the church for no one knew she was there—at least I didn't," Mr. Gaston said.

"Well, the singing stopped. You could have heard a pin drop. It was so quiet. Then Widow Sessions said an unusual thing. She said she knew exactly what she needed to do to get right with the Lord, and she'd already done that. But she wanted the community to forgive her for being so mean all these years. And there was one other thing she needed to do. She asked to be baptized this comin' Sunday in Willoby's Pond Creek."

"I just sat there dumbfounded," Dad said. "It was a miracle. It had to be," he kept saying over and over.

"Can you believe that, John?" Mr. Gaston said. There was no doubt he knew as well as Daddy and everyone else how old Widow Sessions had berated the whole community ever since Mr. Sessions had died.

Dad used to say, "I guess she never got over Clarence's death," giving her the benefit of the doubt. "It seems she always held the people, the church, and God responsible for some reason."

Oftentimes she'd drive her little buggy lickety-split down the road. If you were in her way, you'd best get out, for it appeared she was mad at everyone and would just as soon run over you as not, evidently not caring one way or another.

"Don't be too engrossed in what you're doing or thinking or while eatin' that Babe Ruth candy bar," Mother always cautioned Luke and me if we were on the road and heard Widow Sessions coming in her buggy.

"Just jump out of the way as far as you can get," she'd remind us every time we went to the store for her.

We could hear that old whip she used, slicing the air as it went "whop, whop," ringing in that poor old horse's ears as he did double time on those old country roads. No one ever knew what her hurry was—it was as if she had a mission and the time was now—never considering anyone else.

"The one and only night we haven't gone to that revival and just look what's happened," Mother said sad-like. "I guess them prayers have been answered, John. But how I hate to have missed her being saved and all, and giving her testimony too."

Mother was so disappointed we could tell, but she began thinking what was going to take place the coming Sunday, making us all aware of a special happening.

"If there's going to be a baptizin' this Sunday, then that means only one thing. A picnic on the banks of Willoby's Pond Creek for everyone before the baptizing. That's just two days away, John. I'll have to get busy and make a cake and bake some pies. And John, come Saturday morning you can kill old Spurs (Spurs was our old red rooster). He's been floggin' everybody lately, so it's time for him to go. We'll have chicken and dumplings, that's for sure."

It was about the biggest day I could ever remember at Willoby's Pond Creek. Everyone was there, young and old. As soon as church was over, we all headed for the creek with our food. Tablecloths made from flour sacks stating "Satisfaction Guaranteed" were laid all over the area. Food was placed on the cloths, soon covering up the spaces. It was a grand day. Excitement had extended to everyone, including my friends, Mary, Phoebe, and myself. We walked hand in hand all around, giggling and talking with our other friends and the boys. You can best bet Trevor was there with his family. After lunch, we waded in the creek, waiting for the baptizing.

It was a time we all remembered and would recall years afterward.

After the leftover food was packed up and placed either in the old cars or buggies, it was time for the baptizing. There were several to be baptized that memorable afternoon, but none brought as much excitement as old Widow Sessions' baptism.

She was dressed all in black besides her black robe. The preacher led her out while she held a clean white handkerchief in one hand to be used over her nose and mouth as she was put under the water. All the onlookers began singing:

> Shall we gather at the river,
> where bright angel feet have trod;
> with its crystal tide forever
> flowing from the throne of God.
>
> Yes, we'll gather at the river,
> the beautiful, the beautiful river;
> gather with the saints at the river
> that flows from the throne of God.

Well of all things to happen that day, it would have to be with Widow Sessions. Reverend Liles had one hand on her back to support her, and his other hand over her mouth with the white handkerchief. Just as he started putting her under, his foot slipped on a slippery rock and they both went head over heels into Willoby's Pond Creek. It was so sacred and yet so hysterically funny that you couldn't help but laugh. We didn't want to hurt Widow Sessions' feelings and have her get mad and backslide on the very day she was being baptized, by us laughing.

All of a sudden, the laughter stopped when Widow Sessions came jumping out of the water, shouting all over the field. Seeing how happy she was, everyone began laughing again, clapping their hands, and crying. Two of the neighbors were holding dry towels for her, but no one could get near her long enough to dry her off. The preacher was forgotten about but made his way to the bank of the creek to recuperate. Mr. Liles was teased for a long time about being baptized twice. He did admit that he was only sprinkled the first time. I couldn't help but smile to myself as I stood in the space where the old kitchen once was, remembering the day Widow Sessions and the preacher were baptized real good.

After Widow Sessions joined the church, she was as different as night and day. She attended every meeting that was held and joined the ladies' aid. She also left her money and property to the new Sunday school classrooms and the new lighting fixtures when we finally got electricity. For years, the talk around kitchen tables was about Widow Sessions and the miracle in her life.

Thinking about Widow Sessions brought other happy memories about our kitchen in the old house. The good times outweighed the bad. Mostly our kitchen saw happy times—fun times.

The same oval table and heavy matching chairs that had belonged to my great grandparents sat in the middle of this room. There was a Hoosier cabinet that had a flour bin and roll top door where baking powder, sugar, salt, and pepper were kept. In the corner not far from the cabinet was the hand water pump. That made it real convenient not having to go out to draw water from the old dug well on really cold mornings or just any time.

Sometimes in the winter months the old pump would freeze too. A bucket of water was kept on the stove to be heated to prime the pump the next morning. As soon as this was done, we'd be back in business once again, pumping water for the household.

When Momma got running water for the home, the old pump was taken out and put with the other antiques.

Every Sunday brought someone to our house to eat at our table—mostly uncles, aunts, and cousins. Mother always prepared Sunday dinner on Saturday, or as much as she could. Still, it was a long wait until dinner was served. I can remember being so hungry and wishing the others would hurry and finish. She could fry chicken the best in the world, and her mashed potatoes were so creamy. How good they were with all that butter and pure cream. It's a wonder we weren't fat as hogs, but we never were back then.

Sunday nights were for church and nothing else. Afterwards we came home, starved, eating leftovers (if there were any) from

Sunday dinner. We'd sit and talk until Grandfather's clock bonged 10 times. That was our curfew and off to bed we'd go.

In our big old kitchen, the wood-burning stove set out from the wall. On really cold mornings when we were small, we'd get behind there and finish dressing. It was a monstrous looking thing, with an extra container on one side for hot water. There were two warming ovens at the top with heavy doors. As we got older and became involved in other activities to do from school or church, we were not always there at supper time, but Mother kept our food in the upper warming ovens. Now, I wonder how Mother knew how warm the big oven needed to be for a cake or for bread. But she did—they always came out perfectly.

Thinking about the old iron horse, I want to laugh out loud when I remember the incident concerning our cat, Old Tom. The lock on the oven door became loose and the door wouldn't stay up like it was supposed to unless someone put a piece of firewood or a stick under the door handle to keep it closed.

It was a cool day in the spring of the year. After Mother had made dinner, she let the door down to help warm the kitchen. Sometime that afternoon, Old Tom crawled up into the oven where it was warm for a cozy nap.

When Mother started supper, she closed the oven door, fastening it with a stick, and then built a fire in the stove. She was busy in the kitchen, but she thought she kept hearing the cat meowing. Suddenly she realized the sound was coming from somewhere around the stove. She hurriedly opened the oven door, and much to her astonishment, the cat jumped out. Old Tom didn't waste any time getting out of the oven or out the back door. We teased Mother about that for a long time, and she liked to tell it herself occasionally. We knew it would have hurt her deeply if anything had happened to Old Tom It wasn't long before a new latch was installed on the old oven door. Tom never ventured there again to my knowledge.

As my thoughts continued coming back to me, I hadn't thought about what Mother or I did after the evening meal in a good many years. I wonder how I could have forgotten it. Once the supper dishes were washed and dried, Momma would say, "Jane, you can prepare the table for morning now." Most of the time she didn't have to tell me. It never crossed my mind but that every household did the same as we did every evening. The knife and fork were placed at each setting and the plate was turned over the silverware, each one awaiting the next morning meal. The spoons were always kept in the middle of the table in a crystal glass spoon holder, either inside of it or hanging around it. When company came the spoons were hung all around the container on tiny wire rings attached to the holder.

How did we ever manage with such few cabinets and drawers back then, I thought, as I stood where our kitchen was long ago.

The voices and conversations I could almost detect, as I looked around in the empty space.

"Now, Aunt Mamie, you can sit right here." That was Mother's voice. "We're so glad you got to come again for this occasion."

That was Thanksgiving and Christmas voices I could hear. It was right here that dinner was served, at 1:00 sharp, even if it was a holiday. Our big old table could accommodate eight to ten people. It would be loaded with some kind of meat, not always turkey, but always bread dressing and gravy. Many a year there would be rabbit or pork, sweet potatoes, mashed potatoes, home canned green beans, cranberries, Parkerhouse rolls, and jello made and set outside covered to congeal, for there would be no ice in the box that time of year. And those wonderful fruit cakes made in October, then wrapped in cloth and set down in big containers, kept in a cool, dry place with slices of apple on top to keep them from drying out. The aroma when opened was heavenly.

I could see Daddy sitting at the head of the table telling different stories about some of his brothers and sisters. "Yes sir," he would say, "we worked from sun-up to sun-down. No shirkers back then. If you didn't work, you didn't eat." I often wondered if Daddy ever did any shirking—I'm sure he had to be tamed like everyone else sooner or later.

Now, I can look back and realize it hadn't been many years since Great Grandfather Caleb sat at the head of this table just like my father did when I was a young girl. Yes, life goes on, and you have to accept it, no matter what, one day at a time, just like Grandma said.

To awaken on Christmas morning and feel the expectations awaiting you was a wonderful feeling. I remember laying in bed and listening for their voices. Mother and Daddy would already be up waiting here at the table for us. Their first words were always, "Christmas gift," as I slipped into Daddy's big arms. The room would already be warm, even though it might be cold as blue blazes outside. Then we could hear Luke bounding down the stairs and all of us saying, "Christmas gift, Christmas gift" when he entered the kitchen. Just the simplest of things would please us then. A doll for me or a knife for Luke.

The first Christmas I remember, a red rocking chair was awaiting for me with a dolly sitting in it. My mind was in a whirl trying to figure out how Santa got down the chimney with those things. How everyone laughed when I told them I was sure I had heard him on the roof with his reindeer the night before. And not only that, there were tracks outside around the house. Luke and I had seen them that morning.

Daddy told me several years later a calf had gotten into our yard and had run around and around the house the night before. He had gotten up and put it back into the barn. "Honey, you and that old calf made our Christmas that year," Daddy laughed while telling me.

When we had turkey, Daddy sat by the oven basting and basting that old bird. It would be such a rich, moist taste when at last it was carved and served.

I smiled as I remembered the year we were planning to raise turkeys. We'd have our very own turkey for Thanksgiving and Christmas we thought. Well those turkeys became our friends. We marveled every evening how they would fly to the nearest tree after eating corn and scraps. They would start running, flap their wings, take off, and land in the big hickory tree on the knoll above our house, all on the same limb. We simply fell in love with those birds, watching how easy it was for them to reach their nesting place and how they strutted around day after day.

That Thanksgiving, there was no turkey dinner. We couldn't think of eating one of those birds. Mother eventually sold them and after that bought an unknown turkey ready to roast.

How well I remember in the spring of the year when Dad ordered baby chickens. He'd go to the main post office and pick them up. They'd be in a big flat cardboard box just chirping away. They came by train and then were delivered to the post office.

I'm sure he must have known the exact day they'd be ready and waiting for him. He'd open the box and there were these furry fuzzy little birds so hungry and thirsty. They were given cracked corn and water and soon settled down for the night, ready the next morning for more food and drink. Since it was in the spring of the year and still very cool, they were allowed to stay in the small room off from the kitchen. This was a room used for washing clothes and served as a bathroom only for taking baths, since there were no facilities for an inside toilet. In later years, Daddy took this room and made us a nice bathroom, which made Mother very happy—a real luxury in the early 40s. No more did we have to go outside to the toilet on cold frosty mornings after that.

In a few days, the baby chicks were dispatched to several old hens who took them under their wings and showed them how to survive by finding bugs to eat. Daddy always ordered yellow baby chicks, but somehow there would be a tiny black chicken in the group. He was our favorite. We gave him extra feed and he most always was a rooster. When he was grown, he protected his harem religiously by crowing long and loud, chasing the other roosters away.

Thinking about the baby chicks Daddy brought home from the post office caused me to revert back to my childhood at the tender age of eight when Lucky became a part of my life. I hadn't thought of him in a long time, remembering how dear he was.

Our neighbor had several incubators to hatch baby chicks in. His daughter, Mary, had to turn the eggs every day, so on the way home from school, I would stop to help her.

We watched with anticipation, checking them carefully each time. One day in the cycle of life, the baby chickens began to hatch, all but one egg which was much larger than the others had been.

We still turned it every day, not wanting to give up on this one, especially since her father encouraged us to keep watching and turning it like we had the others. "Sometimes it takes longer," he had said, "but it might be worth waiting for," he promised.

In a few days we hurried out to the incubators on our way from school. Much to our surprise, a dark yellow beak was sticking out from the egg, not a chicken beak but a duck beak.

We laughed and jumped for joy while he unfolded, pecking himself out of the egg. He was so cute after he dried off, with those downy yellow feathers, yellow beak and feet that looked too big for his tiny body.

Mary's dad had found the egg out in the pasture field and slipped it in the incubator to see if it would hatch, just to surprise us, he told us that evening.

Mary's mom thought he should be called Lucky, for indeed he was a lucky duck, instead of a forgotten egg to be trampled by the animals in the field.

As soon as the baby chicks were strong enough, they were given to a hen to be taken care of, and Lucky was included. An old momma hen claimed him as her own right away.

What was so strange was that momma hen would take her brood to the creek each morning. Lucky would jump right in, but the baby chicks would not, of course. He'd swim across the creek back and forth until his momma would cluck-cluck a few times, and out he would come. It was as if she knew he needed his morning exercise in the water.

When nighttime came, their Momma went cluck-cluck until all the babies, including Lucky, would gather under her breast while she folded her wings around them until morning.

He grew up but seemed lonely swimming all by himself. One day his human family bought a new friend for him to be with, a female duck, named Lucy.

The very next summer, she laid several eggs, making herself a nest, sitting on them for well over a month, while Lucky stayed close by, taking his turn to sit on the eggs while she went for a swim or to eat. Six little ducklings hatched, and in a few days, they were taken to the creek for their first swim by Lucky and Lucy.

Oh, the childhood memories I had stored away and so many from that big old kitchen—some of them forgotten until now.

Most of the time our kitchen was like a beehive, humming with activity. Things stayed pretty much the same, even during the war except there was a new little one to be fed and taken care of. Little Trevor began to grow up right here where his mother and the family he knew had done the same before him.

How well I remember the holidays not being the same while Luke and Trevor were gone those two years. We hoped there was food for them, but we also knew there were C-rations, and that's how they survived. Occasionally there was a good meal, but not so many in the cold months of 1943 and 1944 we learned later.

It was fun to watch little Trevor eating the meat from a drumstick in his high chair, while all the time hoping and praying his father and uncle had enough to eat each day.

As I walked in the space where the kitchen used to be, I could picture where the ice box once sat. Daddy's grandfather had put it together. Not a nail was used. Each piece fit perfectly. It had a large section at the bottom to keep milk and butter in. There was a smaller compartment for ice at the top. It was lined with tin that helped keep an even temperature, so the ice didn't melt as quickly.

We didn't always have ice, just in the summer months. Daddy brought it from town each week. There was a space on the back of our car for a chunk of ice to set. I think it was a 1936 Ford, but I can't remember exactly right now. He'd carry that piece of ice into the house and set it down in the top of the ice box. That evening Mother would make iced tea for supper.

As I mentioned before, Daddy had made us a bathroom off from the kitchen in the small room. Luke had taken the old tub sometime before the house burned and installed it in his modern bathroom. It looked so nice with its claw-like feet. I was so glad he had salvaged it along with the wide square-like wash basin.

All at once I remembered there was another space I hadn't thought of. Somehow, in my reminiscing, I had forgotten the place between the kitchen and the back porch, which was aptly called the "Breezeway."

The Breezeway

It was named correctly, for most always you could feel a breeze, sometimes cool or sometimes warm, depending on the time of year of course.

When September rolled around, Daddy and others working for him would start cutting wood for the fireplace and the cookstove. The logs for the living room fireplace were exceptionally large. As I said before, it took two people to heave those huge pieces upon the fire where they might burn for several hours or either two or three days.

The wood after it was cut was brought in and placed in piles in the middle section of the "Way," as we sometimes called it, and tarpaulin stretched across to keep it dry in case the wind blew the rain or snow in which it often did through the screens. It was easier to go to this practically open structure-like room to get wood than to have to go outside in winter weather or deep snow.

Even though the breezeway was nice, most of us preferred sitting on the back porch in the old fashioned swing. Out there you could see into the back yard through the screened-in windows and in the summer evenings, the cool breeze followed the creek down off the mountain, and it felt wonderful after a long hot day, whether you worked hard or played.

As quickly as I had given thought to this space, I left it and the kitchen to other stored away memories, going to another special place in my meditation once again.

It was the back porch. Mother and Grandmother loved this area the most, better than any other spot to be found in this lovely old home.

It must have been this big, I was musing, as I walked from one end to the other. This is the place everyone in our family gathered often, and it is also the place I learned about Grandma one day and the tragedy she had experienced while still so very young.

Reliving it like another yesterday, I stepped onto the back porch as if it was still there, while memories of long ago flooded my mind once again.

The Back Porch

For several days, Grandma and I had set aside this time to sew. She was teaching me to crochet and do some intricate embroidery for my hope chest. I think I was already thirteen years old. Anyway, we chose the back porch because it was cooler there this time of year, which happened to be July. It was just like another room with a roof; where the walls would have been, screen was there all around to let in the cool breeze.

When August rolled around, there would be lots of activity here. That's when the fields would yield their fruits for us to survive the winter months or another year.

The back porch is where all the vegetables were brought in from the gardens. Things were prepared for canning right here. The beans were strung, corn shucked, cut from the cob to be put down in crocks for pickling or glass jars for canning. A barrel was used for small cucumbers placed in very salty brine and covered with a lid made from material just like the barrel. This barrel was always kept in the little room off the kitchen, which later became the bathroom.

While we were preparing to work on my hopeful things, we couldn't help but laugh about Old Tom and Mother's oven where he had tried to take a nap.

"When I was a young girl," Grandma said, "every household had a cat, mostly to keep mice out. And yet, they would get in and sometimes ruin your cherished things." She told me how they had to be very careful of their clothes or anything they had prepared for their future hope chest. We giggled like teenagers, wondering if old Tom had ever caught a mouse in his lifetime, for he was such a house cat.

Grandma had a large trunk that was painted red. I had seen it many times in her home, but had never attached any significance to its place in the world. An old wooden box Mother had given me served as my hope chest. A few days before, Grandma had asked Daddy to bring the red trunk to our house by sled. The back porch would be a good place to leave it for that week she had said, and so Daddy put it there in front of the comfortable old padded swing. As we removed the things I had finished from the old box to the trunk, Grandma began talking.

"When I was thirteen years old, just like you, Pa bought me this old trunk to keep my possessions in. My mother and I began to make plans for the day when I would be married. After the chores were done, we'd sit up and work by lamplight on scarves and pillow cases. We made sure everything was kept in the trunk away from the mice. By the time I got married, I had a trunk full just like you are going to have one day, Jane."

"This old piece has seen many days, some happy, some sad. If it could only talk. I guess I'll have to be its mouthpiece. It's like an old friend in many ways, but one day when I'm gone, it will be yours, Jane."

I dared not interrupt her just then by acknowledging what she was saying or to thank her for a treasure she was planning to leave to me. So I stayed silent while she reiterated her memories about that black day in her life.

By this time I knew my grandfather had been tragically killed while cutting timber. My mother would sometimes say, "I never got to see my father—I wonder how he would have been." But she never lingered over things she couldn't do anything about. She'd often say, "You can't miss something you've never had, but I can imagine how it would be." And with that, she'd change the conversation to something else. My mother was a pleasant woman who laughed a lot and found something good in everyone she met.

Being a cheerful person, she liked to tell the story about a group of people who were criticizing old Jim who lived in the community. Out of the group someone spoke up and said, "I know Jim has his faults and he gets on our nerves, but who doesn't now and then? But I want you to know he can whistle real good." And with that, she would say, "There is some good in everybody. Sometimes you just have to look or listen for it."

This little story always made me think twice when I thought of complaining about someone who didn't live up to my expectations.

And now thinking about Mother, I remember something she did quite often for someone else. She supposedly could cure thrush in a baby's mouth. The old wives' tale went like this:

If you were a girl and your father was killed or died before you were born, you could cure thrush in children by blowing nine times into their mouth while holding your breath. People came from miles around bringing their babies for Mother to blow in their little mouths.

It must have worked. No one ever came back for Mother to re-blow. While the news kept spreading around, the people kept coming. There had to be some kind of medical reasoning, I've often thought, but who knows for sure just how it was accomplished.

She always took the children into her bedroom, not letting anyone watch her. "I don't know how it works," Mother said, "but as long as the parents have faith in me, I'll keep on blowing." Then she would laugh and shake her head, not really understanding this thing that others felt she could do. She took no money for this service; just to see the parents released from anxiety was a joy to Mother. No one had money anyway in the depression years.

Returning to the back porch in my thoughts, it was as if I could hear her saying, "Jane," my grandmother began, "when you get married someday, you must love your husband dearly. In an instant, you can be separated from one another, never to see that smile or those tender eyes or touch those hands again." Some years later, how well I remembered Grandmother's advice when Trevor was missing in action somewhere in Germany during World War II.

Grandma continued, "I was seven months pregnant with your mother when my beloved Luke died. It was hard to lose your husband and be pregnant at the same time. Your Uncle Otis was barely over two, I remember, just a little tyke. It was hard after his death, Jane, but we made it with my family helping me every step of the way."

"The day your grandfather got hisself killed was a hot July day, just like today." Grandma paused for a moment before telling me about my grandfather. She then continued, "I had washed clothes in the old washtub. Washing clothes was a hard task; the water used was water caught and kept from the rain in a big barrel. It took a good part of the day to wash back then. It was so hot, they dried almost as soon as I hung them on the line," she remembered.

"His parents, your other great grandparents, gave us the land on which we built our home. We were so proud of our little Jenny Lind house. Your grandfather, with the help of his brothers and Dad, built it by themselves. There was a nice size kitchen with windows made so they would slide to open or close and one bedroom that held a stone and brick fireplace and a wide mantel that he had hewn out himself from a large tree. We had a back porch with a little cellar built into the hillside. That's where the milk and vegetables were kept, as well as the home canned things such as fruits and jellies."

"We had chickens, ducks, and a cow. Old Bessie, that's what we called her. I haven't thought of old Bessie in a long time. She was such a gentle animal. I milked at mornings and he milked in the evenings taking little Otis with him."

"The evening before he was hurt, we sat on the back porch and talked about the new baby to be—your mother. I can still recall his words that last evening we would ever be together. The sun had gone down and it was such a pleasant time of day."

He began by saying, "We'll build another room as soon as we can afford it. You know, Leah, I hope we have a little girl. I think a little girl would be nice for you. There's just something about a little girl and her mother, he sweetly said as he reached for my hand."

When Grandma was telling me this, I remembered the day at the cemetery when she told Mother that her dad had hoped for a little girl.

"The next afternoon it was," Grandma went on talking. "As I said, I had washed and hung the clothes out to dry and then decided to lay down for a few minutes. All of a sudden the stillness was broken by sounds of a horse and buggy coming up the road, real fast. 'Who in the world was that screaming?' I thought. It was your Aunt Liz screaming at the top of her lungs while driving the little spring-board wagon.

I couldn't help but think about old Widow Sessions when she was telling me about Aunt Liz driving up the road at breakneck speed and hollering as loud as she could.

"I ran to the door as fast as I could get up. What I remember about that day was her straddling over this old red trunk I had set in the doorway to keep Otis from falling out. And her words to me as she all but fell into the kitchen, 'Lear, Lear!' That's what they called me, never Leah, but Lear."

"Have you heard about Luke?"

"I was miles away from anyone. How could I hear about Luke? She must have thought how foolish that sounded, for then she told me that Luke had been hurt by a falling tree and had been taken to the hospital. The hospital was far away, and they had to load him on a big old flat bed wagon. They, the men who had been working with him, made it as comfortable as they could and drove over the bumpy roads to town, which was six miles away."

"He died the next day, never regaining consciousness. My world stopped for awhile, Jane, but then I remembered there were two others to think about. I walked to Pa's that same evening, me and little Otis, hand in hand, never going back to our little house again."

"Your great uncles came the day your grandfather died and loaded up everything in a wagon and brought it to this house while leading old Bessie through the path we had taken to Pa's. I never spent another night in our beautiful little home," she said again.

She began again, as if trying to remember the details:

Aunt Liz stayed until two of the boys came for me. I prayed to God if it be his will, Luke would be alright, but it wasn't his will and he went to a better place, I'm sure.

"Luke's friend and coworker unhitched one of the horses from the team and rode as fast as he could go to Pa's. Well, Pa saw him coming up by Willoby's Pond fast-like, and he had a terrible premonition something was wrong, for nobody ever rode a horse that fast that time of day. The poor fellow was exhausted when he alighted from the horse he'd been riding."

"Sir," he said, visibly upset, "are you Luke's father-in-law?"

"Yes," Pa replied.

"Well, sir, I've got bad news for you and your family," he said, as he told Pa what had happened to Luke, his good friend.

"Pa thanked him and took the young fellow in, and one of the girls gave him cold water to drink and to splash on his face. As soon as he could compose himself, he got up on the horse and rode back to where the men were working in the woods."

"Within two hours, my brothers were at my door to help me over the rocky path we had to take to Pa's. This was considered a shortcut and had been used for years by earlier settlers in that area."

"Like I said, I never went back again. There was nothing left there for me. Your mother and Otis went one time with their aunts, uncles, and friends after they were pretty well grown, but neither one ever wanted to go back."

"For the longest, I hardly remembered his funeral. It was as if I was in a daze; a deep fog it was. I couldn't somehow realize he was gone nor could I cry. Now, I know I was in shock."

"My sisters and Pa insisted I stay in bed for a few days before and after the funeral until I felt I could continue with my life. They took over the care of little Otis; they were so good to me."

"Your mother was born right here, in the left bedroom, at the top of the stairs, the same room you and Luke came into the world in. The same room that belongs to Luke now.

She was a skinny little thing, with real good lungs! Just like Aunt Liz," she added. Grandma laughed then remembering how Aunt Liz came screaming to let her know about Luke being injured that memorable afternoon. "And," she continued, "it was then I cried when I saw our little girl, the little girl he had hoped for, for me."

Grandma then went back to the time right before and after my mother had been born, remembering her family.

"My sisters waited on me hand and foot before and after the birth of your mother. I was well taken care of, as well as your mother and Otis. Somewhere, Pa found an iron baby bed and bought it for me, the same one you and Luke used" (and in later years little Trevor and his siblings, as well as my brother, Luke's children).

"No one had mattresses like they have now, Jane, only feather ones. We made a small one for the little iron bed out of goose down our mother had saved.

"Pa made Otis a bedroom downstairs—the same room that now belongs to you. He worried that his grandson might get up one night, not knowing where he was, and tumble down that long flight of steps."

She was then quiet for a few moments, and when she spoke, I knew Grandma was thinking about their little home, for she said in a wistful tone, "The property Luke and I owned was eventually sold to another family. My father-in-law, your other great grandfather, took care of the transaction, bringing me an amount each month, always in silver dollars, stacked into a long leather pouch. There were two pouches, one filled with money and the other empty. Each time, I'd hand him the empty one and he'd hand me the one filled with coins."

She then continued, "I allowed Otis and your mother to play with those heavy silver dollars. There weren't too many things to play with then, Jane, and they played in this very house mostly in the living room or parlor while I sewed their clothes by hand or did work on the spinning wheel."

"Your great grandfather rode a big reddish-brown horse that was called a bay—with its tail nearly touching the ground. Those dear people, Luke's mother and daddy, went to their graves bereathed from their son's untimely death."

"Most of the time I could see him coming up around the pond and knew he would have a payment for me. If I should happen not to see him coming, he'd go to the front porch and holler, "Lear, Lear, come out. I have a little money for you.""

"He never got off his pretty horse or came in to visit. Sometimes he and Pa would talk a few minutes about politics or their crops, but he never tarried long."

"Just as he was leaving, he would always say, 'Come see us Lear and bring those precious children, you hear? We need to keep in touch you know.' And off he'd go until the next month."

"I did keep in touch with them, but it was so lonely and sad for me to go where my husband had grown up, but we did go often, the children and I."

Then Grandma began reminiscing by saying that Otis could never quite remember how his father looked. But there were two things that stuck in his memory.

"He remembered a man with black hair reaching down in his trouser pocket and giving him a shiny penny after he had run to meet him on a little path not far from a small house with trees all around. The only other thing he could recall was this same man with a pocket fob and coins or charms attached to it on his weskit or vest."

"That pocket fob belonged to his father, your and Luke's grandfather. When he got old enough to be responsible, I let him wear it."

"Otis looked just like his father—with his curved lips, dark curly hair, and dark eyes. Your mother looked just like her dad too, but her eyes were not as dark," she said as she looked at me as if to see a resemblance of her first and only love.

"I've heard your father say you were the spittin' image of his sister, Aunt Jane. And you do look an awfully lot like her, yet I think you look like your grandfather, you and Luke both, except

Luke has blonde hair and brown eyes. On the other hand, you have his dark hair and eyes. Your brother's features are chiseled just like his namesake. My, he is so handsome."

Then she looked at me again making sure she had conveyed her message, all the while folding and pressing down an embroidered scarf into the old red trunk.

As she closed the lid on the last item being transferred to the trunk, my heart felt a sadness which I never experienced before. I never thought older people like Grandma ever had anything to be sad about. They were most always laughing and making things pleasant for us, the younger ones.

It wasn't long after our day on the back porch that Uncle Otis gave my brother, Luke, the watch fob that had belonged to our grandfather. Luke wore it on his vest with the chain hanging looped until it no longer was the style of the day. He put it away in its box in his top dresser drawer upstairs. I'm sure he still has it safely kept with his other treasures of bygone days. He will probably pass it on to his oldest son, Luke Otis, named after his great grandfather, father, and great uncle.

Uncle Otis never married or had a family of his own. He lived with Grandma and did the heavy chores for her—always a kind and good man, just like his father had been.

It was a sad day when he died from scarlet fever. Grandma really never quite got over his death, Mother often said. During his last days, Mother and Grandma stayed by his bedside while his fever raged, bathing his body in cool water and a compress for his forehead.

There was so much that had to be done after his death that no one had time to be sad for long. His mattress and bed covers were burned because of the scarlet fever germ. The rooms were washed down with lye soap. They were indeed thankful no one else in the family contracted the disease. He was buried the very next day. There wasn't time to dwell on the sadness of the occasion.

That day with Grandma on the back porch is just as vivid today as it was then. How I treasure what she told me about Grandpa, and how I felt her grief.

As I stood thinking about the sorrow Grandmother had experienced, I realized then there are days in everyone's lives when you would like to throw up your hands and quit, but as she said, there are others to think about besides ourselves, so we go on, conquering that day's crisis until another comes along, when somehow you find the strength to overcome once again. Grandma was a good teacher, for she had experienced so many heartbreaking things in her lifetime but never gave up her faith.

Grandma lived to be 99. She still loved Grandpa Luke until the very last. While she was not herself, she would call his name—as if he was still right there after all these years. It was a love that bound them together forever. No matter what had happened, their love endured even though one had been gone for over fifty years. She had given us so much of her life. She loved Luke and me dearly, I now know.

A few days after Grandma's death, we were still home on furlough when Mother called for me to come to her bedroom.

"Jane," she said, "I have something that belonged to my mother, and three days before she passed away she asked me to be sure and give it to you."

Going to the chest of drawers, the third drawer down, she brought out a small Coats and Coats thread box, lifting the lid for me to see the contents.

There laying in the small enclosure was a doll with a porcelain head, legs, and tiny hands. Just below the knees were rings painted around the legs to imitate hose or socks, and on the tiny feet were wine-red porcelain shoes with a strap over the top of each foot held together by a painted on button. The rest of her was a stuffed body of arms and upper legs, handmade pantaloons, an overskirt or slip, each with two rows of pleats at the bottom—finished out her undergarments.

This priceless antique was clothed in an old fashioned red-checked dress with three pearl buttons running down the front, with a matching bonnet that held white ribbons to tie under her chin.

I gasped, unbelieving with tears starting to form when I saw this lovely gift Grandma had wanted me to have.

Mother then explained when Grandma was five years old, it was given to her for her Christmas present from her parents.

Things were not easy to come by then since the war had been over barely six years, but somewhere her mother and daddy had found this beautiful little doll for her.

Grandma told Mother that her sisters all had dolls like hers as each came along. "We would often pretend having afternoon teas while we brought our babies to attend. We kept busy, you can be sure, while we were young, just as you used to pretend with your dollies."

She continued by saying, "When your dad and I married and started a home of our own, I took her with me in my trunk, keeping her there safe and sound in her little box. I used to open it occasionally, remembering how my sisters and I loved our dollies. And then your brother, Otis, came along and then you— pretending was no more," Grandmother had laughed.

I asked Mother to keep the doll safe for me until we could return home, once Trevor was retired from service. I'm sure she has her tucked safely away until I can claim her once again. I plan to display her standing on one of those loops upon a mantel somewhere. She will be my Jenny Lind, for that's what Grandmother named her.

As I stood where the back porch used to be in my revery, I could see the land before me. In the distance were the trees, the family cemetery, and the path leading to it. All my relatives, some I never knew, including Aunt Jane and my dearest friend were buried there. This is where we used to decorate the graves on Decoration Day, Mother, Luke, Grandma, and I. The place of the blue jars with roses of all colors set down in them and placed at the head of each grave, lovingly.

Coming from where I remembered the back porch, looking toward the creek, my thoughts went once again to Great

Grandfather driving his horse and buggy around the countryside when suddenly I could see another time, not with a horse and buggy but with an automobile.

There was a young girl and her brother standing on the running boards of an old dusty Ford car, holding on with their hands stuck in the windows that were rolled down so the air could circulate, while that person drove slowly, like in case his passengers should lose their grip and fall off.

Every evening Luke and I would wait on the front porch with anticipation for Daddy coming up around the turn, as it was called then, and also in Grandpa's day. When he blew the horn, we'd take off running to open the gates for him so he wouldn't have to get out of the car, being tired from working hard all day in a factory in town.

There were two gates, one close to the main road and another to separate the farming part of the farm. By having two gates, the horses and cows could go from one field to the other, crossing a small creek, not getting out onto the roadway.

Before Daddy got the new car, he had purchased an old A-Model Ford, on which he was always doing something to keep it running. I usually stuck around while he puttered with this and that under the hood. I remember him showing me how to clean the sediment bowl and spark plugs just right.

One Saturday afternoon, I was standing on the running board with Daddy intent on showing me something he was cleaning when all of a sudden, that old car started up on its own.

I heard Daddy say, "Jump Jane," and jump I did. I couldn't believe my eyes, for that old relic went right straight down through the yard, through the palings, and over the terraced edge stopping just short of the creek that ran between our house and the big open field.

Mother came out running to the front porch to see what had happened, finding the two of us bent over laughing. When she saw the car in its new location, she looked at Daddy in such a strange way that it made us laugh that much harder.

I'm sure he was able to turn it around and drive out of there some way, but I don't remember how that was done. It wasn't long until Daddy got the new-fangled Ford with shiny hub caps and everything modern as could be. (He also had to put up new palings where the car went through.)

He took Grandma and Mother to visit kinfolks in our new car. On the way back, Daddy asked Mother if she'd like to steer the car a little as they got nearer to home. She scooted over close to Daddy, taking hold of the steering wheel and drove into the corner of the house. It did a little damage to the house and car, but that was the end of Mother's driving lessons, I remembered with a laugh.

Still standing where I had marked off for the back porch, looking out upon the pasture field, I could see him as if it was yesterday of long ago. There, too, he was looking at me, the most beautiful horse in the whole wide world with a personality to match, who liked to nudge you for salt, an apple, or a carrot. His name was Prince, black as black could be, with a star in his forehead, a handsome specimen, and like I said, a special personality.

He was just like one of the family, and any time he heard us whistle for him, he'd come running across the meadow, nickering and whinnying as he ran. When the creek was low in the hot summer months, he'd come standing by the gate, pawing and nickering until we drew water from the well, putting it in a tub for him. Prince could do just about anything but talk, we always said.

The neighbors who didn't own a horse asked Dad if they could use him for a few days to plow their farm land. They lived about two miles from us. He evidently didn't like being away from his familiar surroundings, for somehow he got out from their field and made his way to our gate in the driveway that morning.

It was Sunday early, and Daddy went to sit on the front porch while Mother made breakfast. What we heard was Daddy saying, "Well, look who's come home."

Luke and I were so tickled that he had done such a thing that we took off running to open the two gates, climbing onto his back, riding him into our yard, while Mother and Daddy hugged and petted him, as if he had been a lost child.

We turned him loose in the pasture, watching him run the length of the field, coming back and forth, for he knew where he belonged. We thought he was the smartest horse that had ever been born, and we loved him dearly.

After that incident, he was never loaned out any more. We only used him to plow the garden, for he was getting well into years. He had the run of his favorite place, the meadow, close to the barn.

How well I remember the spring I had measles of all things. I got to stay in the living room with only a small amount of light coming in from the drawn green scalloped shades with the little tassel in the middle hanging down. How I hated having the room dark, for it was believed then that measles could cause blindness or weak eyes if you were not kept in a semi-dark room.

It was a welcome relief when Mother came into the room that afternoon, but not when she told me what had taken place that day.

"Jane," she began, "I have something to tell you, and it's not good news. Prince broke his ankle, and there was no way for it to mend. He had to be shot," she continued. "Dr. Moore said he had to be put out of his misery."

"What happened!" I cried out.

"We don't know anything except Luke found him down this morning when he went to milk Old Claudia. Instead of going to school, he went to get Dr. Moore, who even before saw his condition didn't give Luke much hope."

"He came, took a look, petted and talked to Prince. He shook his head with deep sorrow and told Luke he would have to be the one to decide to end his misery."

"Luke went right then to get Old Mac, who is an expert marksman as you know. And I'm sorry, Jane, but sometimes we don't have lots of choices. We'll miss him—he's been around a long time, just like family."

"Your Dad will have to be told when he gets in this evening. What a shock it will be for him too."

"He just went right to sleep," Luke told me that evening after he had prepared Prince's burial place while waiting on Dad to help in lowering him down. "When you get over the measles, I'll take you out in the far meadow and show you where he is. If you'd like, we'll put up a stone and write his name on it."

I nodded that would be fine, for right at that moment, I couldn't speak. And for once, since taking the measles, I was glad the room was dark.

Again Luke was about the bravest fellow I ever knew, for he had to give up another friend, even though this one was from the animal world, but I noticed he stayed out by the barn a long time that evening.

I often heard Mother say Luke had been saddling Prince since he was six years old, by standing on a chair. He and his old friend had been together for over ten years. Prince was just like a true friend, and so was Luke.

Grandma had bought him as a young colt, spending most of his life right here on the farm. He had pulled many a plow in his lifetime, also taking us in our small buggy before we ever had a car. We treated him like any animal should be treated, and in return, he loved us as we loved him.

Yes, we placed a big stone where he was buried, and then Luke took a chisel and carved out his name there upon the stone up in the meadow where he liked to be best of all, it seemed.

<u>The Balcony</u>

I left the back porch, Daddy's old jalopy, Prince, and Grandma's red trunk to my memories, circling where our house once was. I knew Grandma had been married on the porch-like balcony that was above the main entrance like a portico, with French doors opening from the top of the stairs inside onto this fancy setting.

I loved hearing about my great uncles slipping out the French doors at night, straddling the bannisters, skimming down the columns to visit a friend to play cards (which Pa was very much opposed to), attend a dance where their favorite girl might be, or go to another church just to walk their current girlfriend home.

The evening my grandmother was married, people came from all around to witness the happy occasion. In those days, the horse and buggy was their sole means of transportation around the countryside, so the buggies were unhitched and the horses put in the pasture field to graze until the festivities were over. The buggies were parked in the back away from the crowd, for after the wedding a square dance was held with lots of fiddling and banjo playing going on. The day was long, so grain and water were given to each horse.

"On the day of the wedding, about noon people began to gather, for Pa had prepared a barbeque for all. He was a wonderful host, making sure all our friends had plenty to eat. We worked hard getting things ready for that special day, I assure you," Grandma had said with a sigh.

Most of the afternoon the men played horseshoes, clanging the stake, making a ringer quite often, while the girls played croquet.

"How I wish there had been a camera then, Jane, to capture the moments of our wedding. We came out from the French doors upon the balcony while our friends stood in the yard looking up hearing our vows."

"Afterwards we descended the red carpeted stairway, my sisters and the two brothers, who were there at the time trailing behind, coming out to greet our friends and loved ones. It was such a grand day, I shall remember it forever," she told me more than once.

"I wanted your mother to be married there too, but it had become fashionable to be married in the church, so we only had the reception here in the house."

Grandma continued, "I can still see the lanterns hanging on the balcony and all over the yard. Most of the young people danced until midnight, when Luke and I slipped off to get into our buggy, taking off down the road by Willoby's Pond Creek over yonder close to the turn," she pointed to the left.

"But our friends had outsmarted us by tying tin cans to the buggy, which sent us laughing and jangling through the night until we reached our little home which Luke had worked so hard to build."

"My brothers, along with your Grandpa Luke, had moved the furniture into our future home, while my sisters and I measured the windows for curtains. I was not allowed to be there unless my brothers and sisters were with me before we were married."

"Pa had already purchased and presented us with a cookstove, along with a bed that had been in his family for a long time. We had two rocking chairs, a small wooden table with drop leaves, and four kitchen chairs, with lots of odds and ends, including heavy iron skillets, a biscuit pan, and our pretty dishes with the blue birds that are in your Mother's cabinet in the kitchen now. The dishes were a present from Luke's mother and father. We set up housekeeping, happy as larks with our small possessions."

__The Belling__

Grandma went on saying, "Well, Jane, I mustn't forget to tell you about the custom that came from the old world called Belling. In one week after we were married, all the folks around came to our house in the evening for the Belling, as it was called. We knew sooner or later they'd be there hoping to surprise us by ringing bells; cow bells they were or any kind of bell they could find. This was to let you know your friends still cared and thought of you, and this activity was supposed to bring you good luck. And the only way you could get them to stop ringing the bells was to bring out sweets—mostly candy."

"Well, Pa got wind of when they were coming, went to the store, buying all kinds of candy; some licorice and hard-rock, so we were ready when they came ringing those awful bells. It was a lot of fun, and all of our friends got to see our little Jenny Lind home. I guess in many ways it brought us good luck. It brought Otis and your mother, and now you and Luke," she said as she touched my arm. "We didn't have many years, Jane, but they were full, and we loved one another so very much."

With those words from Grandma that I remembered, I left the balcony, Grandmother's wedding, and the Belling Day, finding myself in what was once our back yard.

The Back Yard

There to greet my eyes was the old well, it's tiny roof, bucket, and rope still in place—the butternut tree, and the gooseberry vine. I shook my head remembering how sour those berries were, but how good the jelly was. Standing forlorn, each facing the other, were the two sections of wood that once held the clothesline in place. I wonder how many times Mother had hung our clothes out to blow dry in the wind.

Luke and I used to bat a ball or play marbles here, the thought came to me.

Marbles! How could I have forgotten playing marbles with Luke? He always beat me at the game, and I'd wind up in Purgatory each time. It was hard to get out of Purgatory; even if you did, you could still get shot and put back in.

He'd dig three holes about 50 inches apart and then another called Purgatory at the top, always to the right of the other holes, and if you got in Purgatory, you had to wait three turns to get out.

I'm sure he learned to play at school, for at recess you could see the boys gathered in groups playing marbles all around the schoolyard. His fingers, especially the thumb, were calloused from shooting.

"Come on, Jane," I could hear him say as if it was right now. "I'll let you win one if you'll just play for a half hour or so." I'd get pummeled for sure, but I always came back for more.

He'd even let me shoot first sometimes. Now I know after all this time why. If I made the first hole and got out of there, he could then shoot me wherever I was.

Why had I not ever played a game of marbles with our children? It may be too late to play with them, but I'll teach my grandchildren if we ever have any someday, right here in this back yard.

Yes, this is home, and I need to come back to it. It was like a revelation had been made to me. This is where I belong with

Trevor and the kids. They'd be happy here. We'll rebuild in the same spot. Oh, wouldn't Mother and Daddy be happy. Grandma would be so proud. (We'd be right here with Luke and his family too, once again.)

Just about that time, I heard Trevor coming up behind me, sloshing through the weeds, then touching me softly on my shoulder while saying in a teasing manner the way his parents always talked, "Lil darlin,' I ope to tell you, hit's time we be a' goin." I glanced around me once again, realizing I had come home for sure.

I smiled, looking up at him, knowing that he knew I had made a decision.

"Is that a tear on your cheek?" he asked, as if he was really concerned, all the while smiling.

"Yes," I replied. "I wouldn't want Grandma to be disappointed."

<u>Ending</u>

A friend who now owns where my grandparents lived asked me to come by while on vacation and he would take me where their home once was. I was so happy for the opportunity and seeing the place moved me beyond words.

We traveled in his truck up the rugged road with the creek on one side, trees and mountains on the other. Finally we reached our destination, or as far as we could travel by truck.

We got out, crossing the creek, crouching through a barb wire fence, a grown-up thicket of trees and shrubs, took a deep breath, and began climbing the hill that led to where their little house had been.

Leading up to the site was an overgrown path, and marvel of marvels, there were these beautiful wild roses on each side— roses my grandparents had set out so long ago, I was told.

I couldn't but wonder what they might have thought when planting those beautiful flowers.

I like to think that she thought these will be so pretty for him to see when he returns each evening. And I like to believe that he would think she would see them while busy with their home, or perhaps taking the children for a walk down the path to meet him on his return from work each day. Whatever their thoughts, I felt my grandparents were in tune with one another.

The little Jenny Lind house (Jenny Lind was a famous opera singer during the 1890s) they had built was now just a few dilapidated boards and brick pieces of structure. Imagine my surprise when my friend and I dug out of the ground a whole brick, which had once been from the chimney or fireplace. I brought it home for my children and grandchildren to see.

I could visualize my grandmother washing clothes in an old tub, in water caught in a barrel, using an old fashioned scrub board, then hanging them out to dry in the hot July sun, very much pregnant with my mother. I also thought about the old red trunk placed across the doorway to keep little Otis from falling out. Suddenly, somewhere in the distance, I heard the tinkling of a cow bell and immediately thought of old Bessie.

Along with the silence broken from the tinkling of a bell, I could somehow imagine the clopping of the horse's hooves and the turning of the spring-board wagon wheels coming full speed, up the dry, dusty roadway to alert Grandma, with Aunt Liz shouting at the top of her lungs. "Lear! Lear!"

As I stood before the rotting debris, my heart went back to the events after their wedding day when friends came to wish them happiness and good luck with the old tradition from the old country by ringing of the bells.

In my mind's eye, I could picture pretty young girls in calico dresses, tiny waists, button shoes, and yellow straw hats hanging down their backs made secure by colored ribbons tied in a big bow toward the front, while rugged handsome young men in cotton long sleeve shirts, buckskin or heavy cotton trousers held up by leather belts, serenaded the couple on the back porch with the ringing of the bells, who happened to be my grandparents.

I could see buggies surrounding their home with horses patiently waiting while swatting the evening flies occasionally with their long silky tails.

Standing in awe, I felt the sorrow Grandmother had conveyed to me years ago, while also feeling a closeness that's difficult to explain.

I took pictures of the surroundings, thinking about Grandma wishing there had been a camera to capture the moments of their wedding day.

Tears began to fill my eyes as I remembered my grandparents and how their dreams were shattered in just a twinkling.

It was so peaceful and quiet at that moment, but the shadows were lengthening, letting me know it was time to go.

With much reluctance on my part, we started back down the little path edged with wild roses, the same little path we had taken to get there.

What a wonderful and enlightening afternoon it had been, but now was ending. I felt a mixture of sorrow and happiness in my breast as I realized all things have to come to an end. "But hey, I can come again," I said to my friend, as I brushed a tear aside.

I'm so proud of my heritage concerning those before me. I often think how fortunate I am coming from the roots of these wonderful people who dug and carved out a living and presented me with their best. I will be forever grateful.

At this writing, Grandfather has been gone 106 years and Grandmother 69. Growing up, Grandmother and Mother made their past seem so alive to me. I'm sure this explains the closeness I feel toward them today.

About the Author

Margaret is a native of Charleston, West Virginia. She graduated from Stonewall Jackson High School (the Generals) and attended Capitol City Business School.

In 1953 she and her husband, Bob, moved to Northwest Florida, where they still live. They are parents to five living children, ten grandchildren, and one great granddaughter.

Margaret has written one other book (*Come, Full Circle*), which contains six short stories, three humorous and three serious, depicting the Depression and World War II, with other characters from the humorous side you come to love.

The author is a member of First Baptist Church of Milton, Florida and the Martha Sunday School Class. She is also a member of the Garden Club, Daughters of the American Revolution, and the United Daughters of the Confederacy (two great grandfathers served on opposite sides in the war between the states).

Besides writing, she loves to read, sew (occasionally), and listen to music of the 1940s and 1950s.

9 780759 678682